LOCKDOWN LIAISONS

PRAISE FOR *LOCKDOWN LIAISONS*

'Shobhaa De is the chronicler of our society and its inner thoughts, its outer actions. During the lockdown, she did what she always does — chronicled our society through its many strata, its thoughts and deeds. As she says, this time will thankfully never return, but it has changed so much that we must never forget what transpired now. Her *Lockdown Liaisons* will help us to do exactly that.'

ASHOK CHOPRA, PUBLISHER AND AUTHOR.

'Only a Shobhaa De could have given birth to literary sextuplets, each one perfect — the eyes and the ears, the mind and the heart and, above all, a perfect face. Each liaison is amazing and sublime, sensitive and poignant, timely and opportune, all woven together like a contemporary Bayeux tapestry of India's long lockdown days of fear and pain. It's a paean to those who survived. A requiem to those who could not make it.'

MANJEET KRIPLANI, CO-FOUNDER AND EXECUTIVE DIRECTOR, GATEWAY HOUSE, A FOREIGN POLICY THINK TANK, MUMBAI.

Lockdown Liaisons

Shobhaa Dé

SIMON &
SCHUSTER

London • New York • Sydney • Toronto • New Delhi

A CBS COMPANY

First published in India by Simon & Schuster India, 2020

A Viacom CBS company

1 3 5 7 9 10 8 6 4 2

Simon & Schuster India
818, Indraprakash Building,
21, Barakhamba Road,
New Delhi 110001

www.simonandschuster.co.in

Paperback ISBN: 978-81-946289-5-8

Typeset in India by Mridu Agarwal, Simon & Schuster, New Delhi

Printed and bound in India by Replika Press Pvt. Ltd.

FSC
www.fsc.org
MIX
Paper from responsible sources
FSC® C016779

Simon & Schuster India is committed to sourcing paper that is made from wood grown in sustainable forests and support the Forest Stewardship Council,® the leading international forest certification organisation. Our books displaying the FS ®C logo are printed on FSC® certified paper.

To all those incredible Covid Warriors across the world, who made lives matter, while compromising their own. Thank you, for being our beams of light in a dark and despondent world... the sky belongs to you.

Contents

A NOTE FROM THE PUBLISHER

July 2020

Cocooned in our small little worlds yet living through the most precarious and awful times – this has got to be a first in the collective memory of the whole wide world. Untouched by the footsteps of migrant workers in the hot sun we rave and rant on social media. And as always what helps us to retain our sanity in moments like this are words. Our own words and words from loved ones but even more than that, words from gifted writers who spin stories out of universal experiences, from thoughts and ideas half-formed in our minds.

Simon & Schuster India is happy to bring to you short stories by the inimitable Shobhaa De as she captures the fragile zeitgeist of the pandemic in her own unique way – through stories that don't provide an escape into la la land but rather stories of love that will make you sometimes smile, sometimes frown but at all times understand the subterranean world of shifting human emotions. The author, and her stories, don't shy away from the tremulous uncertainties of the world as we know but rather help us to confront and understand it all, just a little bit better.

I hope all of you enjoy reading the stories in this anthology and remember in these difficult times to be kind to yourselves, to the people you meet in the pages of this book and to those in your life and in the world outside.

Lockdown Liaisons

FOREWORD

Shobhaa Dé
July 2020

Why was I in such a hurry to write these stories? Looking back to THAT day in March, when just about everything collapsed — and the rhythm of our lives took on a slower beat — I recall thinking, 'I am going to die. We are all going to die... this is the end of the world.' It was an overreaction, yes. But at that moment, it was so real — the panic, the accelerated heartbeat, the deep sense of loss and regret... that for the first four or five days, there was a curious numbness... quickly followed by denial. Then came the confusion and a desperate search for something — anything — that made a little sense. Our collective desperation was tangible — it led us to obsessively hang on to random slivers of information. We sought hope and comfort wherever we could find both. The darkness that descended made us into flightless birds, without nests, without any sense of direction. I felt utterly and hopelessly lost. I had never been as disoriented as I was during that grim period of reckoning. Words have always been my security blanket. When all else has failed, I have fallen back on words. Once again, it was words that rescued me... what a debt I owe them.

The stories started to emerge two weeks later, once I had reset my body clock and accepted a few non-negotiables. Starting with my daily routine — something I should have changed a long time ago, in any case. I started sleeping for nine — yes, nine hours — sans guilt. Out went vanity, as my hair roots started to show and I was happy to own them. Out of hiding came my many vulnerabilities — I cried when I wanted, as much as I wanted to. My pace of work? I stepped on the accelerator, though I was warned it was not the smartest option. I read Instagram posts which mocked pandemic productivity, and urged the world to hit 'pause'. I tried. My 'pause' lasted all of two days. The stories wouldn't leave me alone. Writing them down became my therapy, a way to hang on to my sanity. I clutched on to those words as they poured out and made them my lifeboat. I didn't want to be adrift... I needed a safe haven.

The first few stories were raw and rough and savage and angry. Well... they came from an angry space within me! My children were shocked! The abusive language, graphic sexual content and harsh tone didn't sit well with the family. The stories continued to be dark and twisted and merciless and cynical. Once I had reconciled myself to what we know today — the virus is here to stay — my emotions did an about-turn. But I still couldn't get myself to join the global chorus of 'Let

Mother Earth Heal' — I needed healing myself!

By the fifth or sixth week, so many internal battles had been fought and won! I was feeling more on top of my life, while coming to terms with the past. The anger had subsided. I was hearing a different, more reflective voice inside my head. The stories that emerged later are an accurate representation of the upward mood graph — the storytelling altered along with my own state of being.

As of today — and who knows about tomorrow — I am experiencing an unfamiliar calm. At times, it is eerie, at times soothing. It was the sky outside my balcony, and the many skies I have enjoyed in all their glory over the years, that kept me going as I dreamed of happier tomorrows. If I could look up and the sky was still there, it meant I was alive. Such a precious gift!

May we all keep looking up and beyond the clouds and distant horizons... may we continue to dream and imagine a beautiful world. It is out there, waiting for us.

IN MALIBU MANSIONS

I didn't want Shuklaji's 'blessings'... you know what I mean? After all, what had I accomplished? Nothing all that remarkable. I hadn't put my life on the line or anything. Nor had I 'compromised' the job I no longer had! All I had done is what I thought was the right thing at the time. It was an unplanned, spontaneous decision. By standing up for Shuklaji — the 'go to' guy in our sprawling building complex — I had stood up to pettiness. That's it. I am not sure the other mute residents standing around felt ashamed of their own indifference. I didn't see anybody cringe. At least, there was no visible evidence of that.

Shuklaji had been working at 'Malibu Mansions' for as long as the oldest residents could remember. We were a part of the 'original residents', my husband Sajjid and I. These days, most of the young couples were 'rented people', as they were scornfully referred to by seniors. Which meant, they rented the apartments and nobody knew their antecedents. Nor did anybody care. They rented. They stayed for a couple of years. They moved on.

Shuklaji was the one constant in our frenzied lives. A man with no known 'job description', but a man who did all the jobs – from plumbing, to carpentry to operating the lifts, to fixing fuses. Shuklaji was the one stop man all of us could count on during emergencies, big and small. He was so nondescript in his appearance, if you ask me even now to tell you what he looks like, I'd be scratching my head and wondering – he could be short, or of medium height or tall – God knows! Most of us had never 'seen' Shuklaji. You know how it is... We only see important people. And our family, our friends. Those who work for us, even in our homes, are often invisible. Just blurred shapes and blobs we dont pay attention to. Vague forms with voices. That's it – he was just there! He existed! And thank heavens for that great blessing.

If you ask me what exactly he did in our residential complex, I'd be blank. Shuklaji does everything! He has no designation, no uniform, no official duties. Maybe his salary is paid by all of us who live in 'Malibu Mansions', but I am not sure even about that. He lives in someone's vacant garage. That's all I know. Which is why we had Shuklaji's services during the lockdown when no outside services were permitted. I don't even know how much Shuklaji earns.

I asked my husband the other day, but Sajjid dismissed me with a wave of his hand saying, 'Why do you want to know? You are not paying him out of your pocket, right? You stick to your work.' Work! Ha! What work? I had recently lost my high profile, well paid media job as a news anchor. Sacked! Yup. Just like that... after putting in 22 years with the same company. It didn't make me feel any better that so many of my colleagues and contemporaries had also been given the boot. One call from HRD... one short email... boom! It was over.

A much junior reporter had been promoted overnight to headline the show that had my signature all over it. Yes, she was very attractive. She would do well in my old slot. I heard through the office grapevine that Ms. Upstart had taken a 70 per cent salary cut to bag the vacated slot. I thought to myself, I am not that desperate. Let them pay her peanuts, and train a new monkey. I was so done.

It was on that very morning of the unceremonious sacking that Shuklaji had been summoned to our flat on the fourteenth floor to check our clogged plumbing. The flush in the master bedroom was not working. And that can be so traumatic, right? Sajjid told Shuklaji to 'fix the problem'. I didn't like Sajjid's bossy tone and told him so, when Shuklaji was busy checking some defective valve in the loo.

Sajjid looked up from his Apple and said, 'Oh... so, you don't like my tone? You think I spoke rudely to that man? Why don't you make it up to him, then? Make him a cup of chai, give him a big slice of that salty cake you baked...'

I somehow managed to halt my angry words and angry tears. You know why? I stopped myself in the nick of time. Just as I was about to explode and yell back at Sajjid, Shuklaji came out of the bathroom, with a look of triumph on his weather beaten face. 'That man' whose name my husband knew very well, but refused to use, had fixed the flush. Our shit was not going to float up and upset us after all!

I went into the bedroom to find my handbag. I knew Sajjid would not bother to get up and give him a tip. He'd say, 'What tip? That man is just doing his job! Does anybody tip you for yours? Do I get a tip for mine?' That three letter word — J-O-B — had started to gnaw at my insides. I could think of nothing else! And ever since that cold, nasty call from that bitch in HRD, Sajjid had taken to throwing it at me non-stop — I thought it was most cruel and insensitive of him. Funnily enough, minutes before I got my marching orders, I had requested Shuklaji to come and help me fix the washing machine. With no dhobi, no laundry, no staff... and now the prospect of a conked-out washing machine! All this — and no job! Why was I being tested in such a harsh way?

When I heard the doorbell, I was still absorbing the shock of being unemployed, and I didn't hear it ring. Sajjid bellowed from his desk, which was a few feet from the front door, 'Rehana... get the door! What's wrong with you? Gone deaf or what?' I wanted to yell and scream and cry and beat my chest. I wanted to fling a vase filled with ferns at Sajjid's big head. I wanted to attack his face with scissors and blades and knives. I wanted to draw blood.

I had tears streaming down my cheeks, which I'd forgotten to wipe with my dupatta, when I opened the door for Shuklaji. He must have noticed. He said nothing. He paused. And he paused some more. As if allowing me a little time to compose myself.

He kept his eyes lowered and pretended to fix the sanitizer stand at our entrance. Sajjid hollered, 'Rehana! Get that man to fix the washing machine fast... we are soon going to run out of fresh underwear and clean sheets. I have used the same towel four days running... please, pay attention to priorities. I am dealing with some fucked up delivery issues.'

Shuklaji indicated with his eyes shutting and closing rapidly, and his head cocked to one side that it was okay... such things happened in all families ... and that I should not feel bad if he had witnessed something harsh and horrible... a husband-wife tiff. I was filled with gratitude and wanted to express it in some form. A generous tip was all I could think of... I was not the only one financially hit by the lockdown. Surely, Shuklaji had his own money worries and problems.

Sajjid yelled again. 'Rehana put on your mask and gloves... that man is going to be in the house. God knows where he has come from... stop being so careless.' Once again, Shuklaji and I had a brief, wordless exchange. Our eyes meeting in perfect understanding.

Then came the suicide.

Imagine! A young woman allegedly jumped from the 20th floor of 'Malibu Mansions' and died instantly. Shuklaji was the one who found her body lying in the car park. He was also the last person to have interacted with her a couple of hours before she took her life. Sara had summoned Shuklaji to complain of a water leakage problem in her small balcony where she kept her potted plants. The same balcony she had supposedly leapt out of.

Sara lived alone. She was one of the 'rented people'. Sara's world had collapsed during the lockdown. Without restaurants to review and chefs to skewer, what influence did a food influencer have? Besides, posting pictures of lavish feasts had become such a no no! Only insensitive idiots were merrily displaying images of laden tables groaning under gourmet fare. Sara had become redundant overnight. Her job description no longer existed during these bleak Covid times. But then who knows what the triggers were... does anybody ever know? Sara was gone. Poof! Gone!

When the police arrived, it was Shuklaji they wanted to interrogate first. Sara stayed in a compact apartment in the adjoining tower. Ours was the sort of impersonal building society in which nobody interacted or made friends. Nothing much was known about Sara except that she was a popular food blogger and influencer. Sara used to be featured regularly in the media for being the It Girl of Eating Out. It was said she could make or break restaurants and chefs with a single post. Attractive, successful and always in a tearing hurry, I used to run into her at the gym downstairs and exchange high fives. That was it!

I watched from our balcony as an ambulance drove in. The police were at it, questioning Shuklaji relentlessly. And he was answering calmly, given his inherent dignity. Sajjid joined me in the balcony and stared glumly at the small crowd that had gathered around the police van and ambulance. Social distancing had been temporarily forgotten, as I watched some of our neighbours crowding around, adding to the chaos.

I decided to go downstairs and find out what was going on. Sajjid shouted out, 'Rehana, don't get involved, okay? It is none of our business! We didn't even know that woman.' Again those deeply insulting terms – 'that woman', 'that man'. I ignored Sajjid, pulled on my mask, wrapped a dupatta around my shoulders and waited for the elevator.

As I walked towards the crowd, Shuklaji saw me approaching and greeted me with his usual 'namastey'. When I reached him I noticed tears in his eyes. Tears! In Shuklaji's eyes! But why?

'Madam… do you know this man?' the investigating officer asked brusquely.

'Of course, I know Shuklaji. He has been working here for years and years,' I said.

'We need to question him… he was the last person to see Miss Sara alive. And he was also the first one to discover her body.'

I removed my face mask briefly, to allow the officer to see my face clearly. His hands shot to his forehead, as he 'salaamed' me and said, 'Sorry madam… I didn't recognise you with the mask on. Madamji, please understand, we are only doing our job.'

I told him I was ready to sign whatever statement he required about Shuklaji, and vouch for his character. The cop said, 'Thank you, madam. I asked the other residents, including Miss Sara's next door neighbour. They all said the same thing, "We don't want to get into this police lafda. It could be a rape-murder chakkar... these days, you never know... people are desperate... there is so much danger... best not to let any unknown person enter the house".'

Unknown person? Shuklaji? Was he 'unknown'? I looked at Shuklaji... once again we fell back on the language of the eyes we both understood so well.

He stuttered, 'Bas... aapki dua, Madamji... aur kuch nahi chahiye.' Nobody likes lafdas. Even I hate lafdas. But this lafda involved Shuklaji. And I was prepared to fib that I was still working as an anchor for the television channel that had fired me. I would deal with Sajjid later.

LEAVING

I didn't want to leave Suman behind, when all the others from my village decided to walk home. Our lives were 'sold' to construction sites and the chutiya contractors who bought us. We were no better than ghulams. We worked mostly in Mumbai, but I had also worked on sites in and around Pune. When this Chinawali bimaari hit us, I was not bothered. I laughed when other men on the site started talking about running away from Mumbai and going back to the gaon. Were they crazy? Gaon? Who would feed us? We hadn't got our wages this month, and the chutiya was saying he would be delaying the payment because of some bank lafda. I was willing to stay back and take a chance with this corona-varona.

When everybody else on the site had been bitten by mosquitoes and got dengue, nothing had happened to me. I was a majbut, strong fellow. But my wife called me home. She kept crying, and saying the children were wailing because they thought their father was going to die in Mumbai. I was certainly not going to die. But… I didn't want to leave Suman

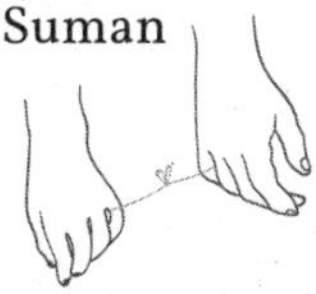

alone and go back to Bihar. Who would look after my woman if I left? I felt sorry for Suman. She was a good person… and we had developed feelings for each other after a certain incident.

Suman worked on the same site as I did, because our labour contractor was common. We both hated his guts. Everyone hated the Seth. When he drove to the site in his shiny car, all of those of us who had suffered his anger and been kicked, slapped and punished by him, wanted to attack him… teach him a lesson, once and for all. Saala haraami number one — if we all left his naukri, who would build his towers? He and his kuttas were heartless… but that was life in a sheher. He needed us and we needed his wages. Sometimes, I was tempted to bludgeon him to death with those heavy marble tiles we fitted into the bathrooms of the saablog who bought these glittering flats for crores and crores.

Suman and I were not the only ones he abused. This particular contractor had a nasty reputation of abusing everybody — he got away with it because he was the pet dog of a neta — the local MLA. Funnily enough, it was his abuses that had made our relationship grow — Suman and mine. It was a day that I will never forget — I think Suman was having her monthly woman trouble, and had taken five minutes off to rest on the side of the cement sacks. The women carried the sacks in a single row, to the men who then transported them to the floor that was under construction.

It was a particularly hot day, and Suman may have fainted briefly. Whatever it was, I saw Mehtaji walk up to her as she sat on the rough ground, with her head resting on her knees. Her eyes were closed, and I could see perspiration pouring down her back. He stared at her for a minute and then nudged her with the toe of his polished shoes. When she did not respond, he roughly grabbed her by the hair and raised her face, 'Aurat! What are you doing sleeping on my time? Do I pay you to come here and fall asleep? What were you upto last night that you are so tired at work? How many men did you fuck, huh?'

Something happened to me when I heard those words, and I rushed like a mad bull towards both of them... I was not thinking! The other men did nothing . They stopped working and silently watched the tamasha. Some of them laughed. Some women also laughed. But I was not laughing — I wanted to kill that man on the spot. That was my reputation in the village as well, when I was much younger. People said I was too hot headed. I would argue and get into fights with the village elders and boys much bigger in size than myself. By the time I was twenty, I looked like an ox. My neck was strong and my shoulders broader than the akhada pehlwans'. People kept out of my way and left me alone.

I ran away from that lousy life after talking to a man who was visiting his in-laws and worked in Mumbai on construction sites — like the one I work on now. Thanks to him, I soon found somewhere to live — in a place called Dharavi. I didn't care that it was over crowded, cramped and filthy — I was in Mumbai! That's all that mattered. Yes, I had left my young wife and two sons behind. I would send them money when I made it. Till then, my parents, uncles and cousins would take care of them.

I was lucky, given my build, I was picked up by contractors phataphat and soon learned how to get ahead on these sites, where we were paid daily wages — just enough to eat two meals and pay the rent of the kholi. I got a little extra for working harder and for longer hours. I had built a good, solid reputation for myself. Nobody dared to act funny with me. Everyone knew about my hot temper and kept their distance. Even the Sethlog showed more respect and generally avoided gaalis when they talked to me. But yes, my charging at Mehtaji came as a shock even to them. Nobody attacked powerful, ameer men who fed them. It was said it brought bad luck to hit someone whose salt you ate. But I could not just stand there like an impotent man… or a hijra… while a woman was being ill-treated.

Mehtaji was too taken aback to react — but everyone saw his expression! His face had turned white and he was shit scared as my fist came close to his face. Nobody moved. I bellowed, 'Leave the woman alone… stop… or I'll kill you.' He froze. And yelled for his security guards. Fortunately, one of them was from Dharavi and lived one lane away from my place. He swiftly intervened and calmed Mehtaji down. I walked away… slowly… towards the gate… without looking back. Suman struggled to her feet and followed me out, walking swiftly till she caught up with me.

We spoke to each other for the very first time, standing under a large peepul tree. We have been together since that day. Now the time had come to join the others from my village, who had decided to walk home to escape the bimaari. Dharavi was sealed off, and there was a sense of dread, as if death was waiting to enter each gully and take us one by one. There was no construction work. Our money had run out. The police were not allowing us to leave those small rooms, even to use the toilet more than once a day (we had to pay Rs 2 for that!). If we stayed here, we would die of corona. If we walked home, we would die of starvation or heat stroke. Most preferred to take the chance of walking home. I too was ready... but how could I leave Suman behind? If I left for my village now, I was sure I would never come back. I had seen life in Mumbai. It was cruel and without the slightest remorse. Being poor was not an option here. And the virus was at my doorstep now. But how could I leave Suman behind? What would happen to her without my protection? She was a young widow. I had seen others eyeing her. Including the bada-bada Sethlog in their big-big cars. She would be consumed by any one of them, in one big gulp. They stayed away from her because of me. I was not a leader or anything, but even the unionwallas were scared of my temper and didn't do any masti — no tricks — for they knew I would not hesitate to break their jaws.

I looked around my kholi. It contained very little. I had no possessions as such. Just a small cloth bag with two changes of clothes. And I had a cell phone — a good one. New. Not second hand. Suman's cell phone was very old. We could not speak on it properly. If I left her behind, we would never hear each other's voices again. I could give her my phone, but then what would I do on that long walk back to my village if there was trouble? I had heard from others and seen it for myself on television, that workers on the road were being beaten up and sent back. Some of them had died in road accidents — just like that. 'Maut' was a mysterious visitor — no advance warning. No invitation.

I had also seen what happened to workers who were walking along railway tracks to avoid the police beating them on highways. How were they to know that some trains were allowed and some were cancelled? They slept on the tracks with trust in God and hope in their hearts. But I was not stupid and ignorant like them. I was going to stick to the highways and walk with a group from my village. Some people from Dharavi who had more money were escaping in trucks and lorries, auto rickshaws and Ola cabs. Whatever little money I still had, I wanted Suman to have it.

Dharavi was going to be sealed soon. People were saying this was our only chance to get out, before Dharavi was turned into the world's biggest prison. I had seen the *muncipality* babus going from kholi to kholi checking people for fever. They looked very odd in plastic suits from head to toe. I had a few extra masks and gloves which I would leave for Suman when I left. I couldn't bear the thought of leaving her. She had captured my heart. She spoke Marathi, which sounded like music. And her voice was soft, like her eyes. Her hands were rough because of the work she did. And she had a big scar on her forehead, where her dead husband had hit her with a stone. Each time I looked at the scar and touched it with my fingers, my blood boiled at the thought of anybody raising a hand and striking this woman. Had the man been alive today, I would have killed him with an even bigger stone. Good thing he died in a gutter. Bloody chutiya... bewdabaaz.

I used to drink also. Till I met Suman. I realised she would feel scared of me and shrink from my touch if I smelled of gaunthi liquor, which all of us working on these sites drank at night to fall asleep before another day started. Before our ears got accustomed to hearing the abuses of the contractor. I saw the persons in the next kholi putting their belongings into a small tin trunk. Some cooking things were placed inside a steel balti. They had three small children. I asked how will the children manage? It was going to be a long, long walk of over 1,000 kilometres. They raised their hands to the sky and said, 'Allah will look after us.'

Two days later, they came to say 'Khuda Hafiz'. They were smiling. So were the kids, who looked excited. 'First we will try at the bus station to get into a truck. We will sell my wife's gold bangles to pay for the journey. We were told special trains may also start. But by then, we may be trapped inside our kholi.'

Dharavi is the most dangerous place to be, TV-wallas are saying. I still haven't told Suman I am also leaving. I don't have the guts! How will I be able to look into her eyes when I say those words? I lack the courage to inform her. In my village they used to say I could wrestle with a wild boar and win. But in front of Suman, I become a meek rabbit. Even though she never fights or raises her voice. Maybe, I will sit in my kholi for a day or two and think about the best way to break the bad news to Suman. I have the kholi to myself now — the others have left for their villages. They said they were never coming back, no matter what happens.

I am confused. There are no jobs in the village. There is no money. No food. How are we to live? If I abandon Suman, she may die of starvation — as it is, she is weak. She told me she had been to a hospital once and the doctor had told her she had TB. I was not scared of getting TB from her. I wanted to keep her safe and see her happy. Suman had nobody to turn to. Her dead husband's family had disowned her and taken away the kholi she shared with him. Her own parents were dead. Her only sister lived far away and they were not in touch. Suman had a strong mind but a weakened body. Her wrists are as thin as neem twigs. And I know she is very scared of this new bimaari, because that was all everyone talked about.

At one point I got sick of discussing corona and all that. I told Suman to stop thinking about it. Nobody really knew what it was. People were talking kuch bhi. I have stopped watching news on my phone. What is the point? More and more people are dying, left and right. This corona bimaari spares no one. I heard Mehtaji also has the bimaari. He is blaming us! Saying all these dirty fellows from the slums are giving corona to ameerlog! I feel like saying, 'Good! You deserve it.' Nobody from the outside world wants to enter Dharavi. As if corona has taken a permanent kholi here. People are saying soon there will be no place for anybody in hospitals, not even for rich people. But for us poor people, whether we die on the road, on the railway track or in a hospital — it makes little difference.

Though if I die here, who will be there to claim my body?

Cremate me? They won't give my corpse to Suman, if she goes and says, 'He is my man.' They will ask for proper papers and all that. Considering all these things, it is better I go back. I will take my final decision later.

Today, I have kept a nice, ripe mango to give to Suman — the fruitwala gave it to me yesterday, saying, 'Better to give these mangoes to neighbours since, in any case, I can't sell them in the mandi this year. Who will buy fruits from Dharavi? Eat quickly, before the fruit rots.' Suman will be so happy when she bites into the golden mango. I will tell her about my plans to go back to the village, after she has enjoyed the mango. Maybe...

AFTER THIS, DUBAI?

See. From the day we decided to get married, I had told my hubby, 'No kids!'

I liked my life, my job, my friends... I didn't want to be stuck at home changing nappies. He agreed. Then he cheated. Usual tamasha – no protection. This happened after a wild Lokhandwala party. Saturday night, yaar. Everyone binge drinking! And everyone ends the night with sex.

By the time we got down to it, I also got careless and said, 'Forget it... kuch nahi hoga.' I used to work in television – script writer types. Such stupid lines are common on the sets – I used to hear them all the time, and wonder, if these TV stars are bonking non-stop, how come they don't get pregnant? And here I was having a bloody baby, in the middle of Season 3.

I told Anirudh, 'Yaar... this is not fair.' But he made all those silly faces men make when they have zero arguments left... and you know the rest.

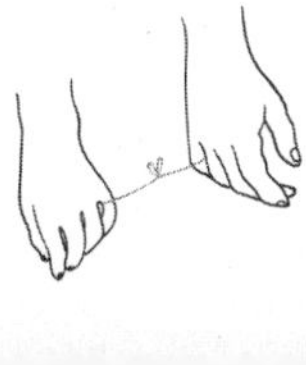

Now... it's day 39 of the fucking lockdown. My baby is one year old and teething. I have just been told I no longer have a job. The television business has been so badly screwed... let's not go there. Anirudh is a journo. His bosses called and told him to take three months off — after that, the management will take a call. Which is another way of saying

'You are fired!'

Life sucks. But at the moment, I am very angry. With Anirudh. Had he not been selfish and used a condom that night, we would not have had Natasha to worry about during this fucking pandemic. We would have managed, somehow. Such a fucking asshole! We hardly exchange a word anymore. I see him on that bloody couch all day, playing some idiotic game or the other. Nobody calls. Well... nobody phones me, either! Even requests for Insta Live have dried up — people know nothing is going on as far as new projects go.

I have so many sexy ideas for a new series... but where's the fucking money to make anything? All those telly stars who would WhatsApp 24x7, with meaningless stuff like, 'Hey Sweetie... lovely DP! Keep me in mind if you're working on something.' And then those emojis! Ufffff... But I miss even that rubbish. Now it's making sure Natasha doesn't stick her baby fingers into sockets. Since we had a no-baby deal — or so I thought — our flat was not baby proofed. Now, who'll come to our building during this madarchod lockdown?

Anirudh won't get off his fat butt (yes, it's fat, and getting fatter) to even stick tape on the ground level sockets. Maybe he wants the baby to get electrocuted? No, that's mean. He loves Natasha... sort of. Maybe he is hoping I will get electrocuted. Naah... then who will cook and clean for this jobless oaf? I told him yesterday, 'Why don't you write a daily blog, like some of your journo friends? See how active they are?'

He glared at me and yelled, 'And why don't you shut the fuck up?' He has not written a word all these days — I find that annoying. Anirudh is a lousy husband, but a good writer. He was one of the five 'stars' in the office. People admired him for his clean copy and good writing style. How can he not want to write? He was born to write!

For me, it's different... I am not talented or anything. Just efficient and hardworking and ambitious. But Anirudh is an original! I said under my breath, 'Writers write even during lockdown.' He heard me and threw his baseball cap on the floor to show his disgust. It's true! I see so many interesting poems and posts from his office people — they are not sitting idle. They have wives and husbands and parents and kids. Everyone is fucking coping! But not in our home!

I actually heard him say to his buddy who also lost his job, 'Husbands are not getting their due — as if we have created this bloody virus!' I shouted loud enough for Samir to hear, 'Neither are wives, okay? So shut the fuck up!'

Natasha started howling and before she threw up her

porridge, I ran to pick her up. Naturally, I forgot about the daal I had left on the gas... how many things could I handle?

'It's fucking burning...' Anirudh hollered. But did not enter the kitchen to turn off the gas. Let the swine eat burnt daal for lunch and dinner. Or cook something for himself. I went into the bedroom with Natasha and shut the door.

The bills were piling up. We had taken a hefty loan to buy this apartment. It was my idea, so I cannot blame Anirudh. I had said at the time, 'We cannot live in some rented flat... it is important to project the right image. Especially in my business. You journalists can get away with your fatela lifestyle and those outdated jholas. But television works differently. I need a good car and a good home to show people we are doing well.'

Our BMW loan was also bothering me a lot. With no income coming in, we were going to DIE paying off these fucking loans. Anirudh was going to blame me, for sure. He used to say, 'I don't need shoshaa — my writing speaks for me... but in your superficial world...' And I would stop him, 'Aeeeeyyyyy... shut up about my world, okay? I earn twice as much as you do.'

He was bound to throw that at me. This fucking lockdown! I would have to borrow money from my Dubai Jijju — but even he was tight for funds — Dubai was as bad as us during this corona-thing. And he's in the construction business! My sister was saying they have cancelled all their vacation plans this year. Poor thing! She used to be so jealous of me, saying, 'My, my… what a glam life you lead! Meeting all these singers and stars.'

I let her think that — though, in reality, I hardly met any star — I was mostly stuck inside the office. She also thought I was well off by Mumbai standards. Now… to ask her husband for a loan would make me look so small.

Anirudh had no money. I had married him for his intellect. He had a fan following in media. That's how we had met. He had come to my office to do a story on my boss lady. I was asked to sit in for a while since a photo shoot of a pitch was a part of his story. Our eyes met — and that was it. Two nights later, we had fucked after a drunken bar crawl around Andheri. We started dating and God knows why, we stupidly decided to get married.

Our shaadi was quite a media event — I invited a few telly stars and entertainers — and naturally, we made it to several websites because of that. One old timer from Bollywood, who was in her early sixties, had also attended, because she and I were salon friends, and we shared an eyebrow threader. I was happy to see her — she had come dressed like a bride herself! You know, jhumkas, maang tikka and all that.

Sweet, I thought. But Anirudh had laughed and mocked her. His conceit was attractive in the beginning… but after a while, I saw through all his maha lagaao tactics. He was just a small town guy, with nice hair and a way with words. I was a pucca Mumbaiwalli — born and brought up here. You know, those smart types — we can do well in any city of the world once we make it in Mumbai.

But it was only when the lockdown happened and we were stuck with the baby at home, that all these things started to bother me. I really couldn't see us growing old together — no way. This lazy man with his fat bum and unhygienic habits that would only get worse over time. I was particular about cleanliness — and the lockdown made me doubly aware of how important that is. If I told him to wash his hands before touching the plates, he would snap, 'Back off, cow!'

Cow? Me? I did Pilates and hot yoga — my body, even after Natasha, was toned and bloody fucking good! People at work couldn't believe I had a one year old! So many guys hit on me when we went clubbing. Forget all that. What bothered me was his sloppiness in the loo and the way he threw his stuff around. Seeing his underwear on the sofa drove me insane. He said, 'It's my underwear... I am free to throw it anywhere and keep it handy.'

Handy? Then he said, 'Thank God I don't suffer from OCD — like you.' So now, my good habits had become a disorder?

I am not sure how long I'll be able to keep my cool if the lockdown doesn't lift soon. I have started sending out resumes, even though nobody is hiring. I am also thinking of a Plan B. Maybe, I can start my own consultancy? Or represent telly talent?

I'll talk to Jijju. Once Dubai opens up fully, there will be opportunities there as well. I just want to get away from this bum. But first, I need to talk to Jijju. I may be wrong, but I think he has always had the hots for me — he had touched me inappropriately during his wedding, but I had put it down to all those shots he had downed. I think my competitive sister senses something, but she'll never admit it. But Jijju, I know for sure, will welcome my move to Dubai... it's a chance worth taking. Besides... there is really nothing left for me here. The virus has killed the woman I once was.

LITTLE, JOYFUL THINGS

I loved dancing. He couldn't dance. I loved singing. He couldn't sing. I loved birds. He was put off by them. I enjoyed colour and clothes and textures and plants and flowers and water bodies and gulmohurs and sunsets and moonrises and stars and perfumes and books and mountains and laughter and fairy lights and nice table settings and candles and breads and seasons and lilies and all sorts of silly things. They fascinated me. But none of this interested him.

I once asked, 'What interests you, in me?' And he laughed like I had cracked a joke. I felt very hurt because for me it was a really serious question to which I wanted a serious answer. A thoughtful answer. I asked him again.

And he replied, 'You never refuse me sex. You give it when I want it'. That was his answer! I was stunned. Was I no more than just an opening in a soft wall? I tried again.

Not immediately, of course, but after a few days. 'Tell me

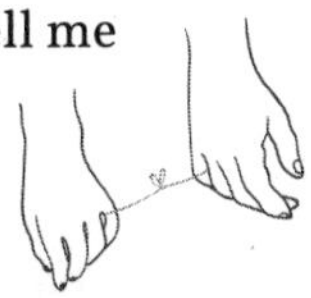

frankly, when you think of me, what exactly comes to your mind?'

He answered promptly, 'Your downstairs thing.' That's it? I asked. Nothing else?

He looked up from the newspaper, his expression was one of great irritation, 'Why do you ask such stupid questions? I am reading an important article written by a Nobel Laureate. Now my trend of thought is broken.'

Aah. I never refused him sex. But come on... sex during this awful lockdown period? Was he totally bonkers? Who has sex during this ghastly period? I had unwashed dishes and a pile of unironed clothes on my mind! Not sex! Besides, had he said what he said sweetly, and with tenderness... even if he had been lying blatantly just to have sex at that instant, I would still have obliged. I thought about our love making — minus any love. Had he never observed me while he was at it? Me! Us!

I recreated our too-many-to-count sexual 'contacts', can't call them anything else. Let me start. Did he notice my eyes? Tightly shut. My mouth? Dry. My forehead? Creased with anxiety. My legs? Wide open. Because I didn't want to waste more time. Every fibre of my being at that moment would be giving out the same message: Please dear God... let this ordeal be over soon. That was then. During 'normal' times. This was now! When we were trapped. And I was bone tired and brain dead.

Did he not sense my utter lack of interest? How's that possible? He's a pretty sensitive man. He prides himself on his immaculate taste in the fine and beautiful things in life. How could this same man not notice my tears when he lay on top of me, his face just a few centimetres from mine? Did he not observe my haste in 'getting it over with'? Did he not care I never ever touched his organ? Or the few times when he forced me to, I did so with barely concealed revulsion. That revulsion was multiplied many times over during this pandemic thing.

Yes, once he had asked me in an off-hand way, 'Do you enjoy sex at all?' And not waited for my answer. Another time he had looked up between mouthfuls of ghee rice and said, 'You must be a lesbian. Yes. I think so. Have you ever... you know... with a woman?'

I had laughed self-consciously and changed the subject. But that remark had made me wonder. Maybe I was a lesbian, and didn't know it. Maybe at some point in my life I would find out. But for that, I would have to meet a woman who attracted me sexually and who was attracted to me. Where would I meet such a person?

My life revolved around my husband's life. I did not find his life interesting at all. Because I didn't find him interesting. Now that we were stuck together 24x7 this became crystal clear. We had zero things in common. I think this happens to a lot of women, but they don't admit it. I am sure my own mother did not like my father. I could tell. But my grandmother definitely loved my grandfather. She would touch his face so tenderly, even when he was so sick and lying lifelessly on a hospital bed. I had never seen my mother touch my father. Just as I never touched my husband. There was no need! Touch him for what purpose? He also never hugged me or caressed me. In fact, the only time he touched my body was when he wanted sex.

The day he touched my hand as I served him daal during dinner, I knew I would be under him that night. It is true, there were times when I too experienced pleasure during intercourse. But my pleasure had nothing to do with him. I would enjoy an orgasm on my own! Sometimes because it was a particular time of the month and at other times because inside my head I was seeing a different movie from the one I was acting in at that moment. In my imaginary world, anything was possible. There were no taboos. I could be with one man or many. Or I could be with a man and a woman, or many men and many women. I heard those sort of things were called orgies. I liked such fantasies. Occasionally, I would imagine having sex with animals also. Maybe I was a pervert. But there was nobody I could discuss this with. And that left me confused.

I nearly brought it up with him when he was sprawled out on the couch watching some Turkish series on Netflix. Thank god I kept quiet. He was in a lousy mood because the takeaway pizza guy had turned up really late. And I had not cooked dinner. Our building society was also being really sticky about delivery guys, saying they were spreading the virus and we should all be cooking our own food. I didn't agree at all. I mean, I could be a carrier, too. And I wasn't a delivery boy. So mean to target these people. Anyway, I kept mum about my fantasies. His reaction would have been, 'Are you serious? You want to fuck the neighbour's dog? That Rocky? Maaaan... you are so sick!' I ask you — who decides the definition of sick? I think he is sick to want to bed a woman who shrinks from his touch.

I kept feeling there has to be more to sex than what I was experiencing in my marriage. I also felt that I needed to find out for myself what else there was which I had zero knowledge of. Was I going to die not knowing anything but this awful experience? One day, during yet another dull Covid afternoon, when he was staring at a football match on television without really watching it, I asked casually, 'Do I satisfy you sexually... Or do you miss something in particular?'

Maybe my timing was off. I had accidentally burnt our quinoa with broccoli when he had actually wanted Thai curry with black rice. I was shitting bricks and about to tell him when he shouted 'Goal!' and pretended he had not heard my question. I repeated it loudly this time, and he glared, with his bulging eyes bulging even more. I got scared and left the room. I was hoping the lousy meal would put him off sex. But guess what?

That night, as he dug his elbow into my waist and suggested with his eyebrows that I should lift up my nightie, I decided to lie. I told him my monthly period was on and that I was suffering from terrible cramps. He didn't believe me and demanded proof. I found that very insulting and refused to let him examine me — you know, like the way doctors do when a woman goes for check-ups during pregnancy. He roughly shoved me aside like I was a bundle of the dhobi's unwashed clothes.

This was too much. I screamed, 'You are an animal. You can't dance, you can't sing… you are useless.'

He sat up in bed and bellowed, 'Why didn't you marry a bharatnatyam dancer or a roadside singer if you wanted a husband to entertain you… all this nautanki nonsense. A man and a woman marry to be comfortable. To live in harmony. Not to sing and dance. Understand?'

I wanted to tell him to just give himself and me a chance to enjoy something together – something beautiful and pleasing. A monsoon raag… a walk in a forest… a simple meal shared from the same thali. Was I expecting too much? Or was I actually settling for too little?

But I kept quiet and shook my head penitently, 'You are right, ji, life is not about naach gaana. And I am sorry I lied to you about my monthly period. If you still want to… I will undress… and we can carry on with your plan.'

He smiled broadly. After a long time, he appeared pleased with me. I also smiled back, even though the smile was missing from my heart. I decided I would wait. Tonight was not the right night for decisions. I needed to prepare myself better. Where would I go? No travel, no transport, no flights, no interstate buses, no cars on the roads, no trains — except for migrants. But even though I knew I was stuck... I still did what was needed.

I packed away the fairy lights I had bought with so much enthusiasm from the local market. I put away my volumes of verse — from Rumi to Kaifi Azmi. I would not be needing them for a while. I was packing away my dreams and memories and hopes as well. At least, for the time being. Till I could look up at the sky again, and hear a koyel sing, heralding the rains. What a loss, I thought to myself, staring at my husband's prone figure as he snored in deep sleep. There was so much he could have learnt from me... little things, joyful things.

Our lives would have been enriched and happier. Why did he think my little quirks and habits were only for me? Had he been open to receiving and sharing pleasant experiences, his life too would have improved. Which human being does not enjoy music! Why did he stick his fingers into his ears to shut out the melodies playing on my phone? How could music anger him? It took me a while to understand. It was not music that angered him. It was me. After some time, I understood more — it wasn't me that angered him. It was him! He was constantly angry! Why did I blame myself for his anger? He was not the only angry person during the pandemic. The whole world was angry. Having sex calmed him down temporarily. That is why he needed it frequently, like some people need blood pressure tablets. I didn't want to be his tablet. I wanted to be his loving wife and partner. I wanted to share his life. Not his prescription.

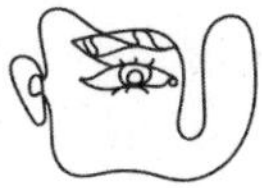

RASAM AND WEED

I had fallen for her because she was nuts. Nuts, in a nice way. I enjoyed her nuttiness. I mean... she was the one who had suggested a wedding in Ladakh... at a time when only serious adventure seekers went there. I hated the idea but said okay, because I didn't want to sound boring and gutless. My parents were most upset and said they would not attend. Nor would any of our relatives — most didn't know where Ladakh was. Which was the main reason for picking it!

I was the first son of my family — the only son. I was christened 'the golden boy' by my grandfather, while my mother called me 'Gopal' referring to Krishna, our family deity. My girlfriend — now wife— was wild and wonderful.

When I brought her home to meet my parents and sisters, she said, 'I keep changing my name periodically, because I don't like being trapped in any sort of box — caste, community, religion, language... so feel free to call me by any name you choose.'

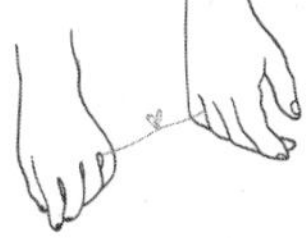

My mother and father exchanged looks and said, 'Please wait... we need to think.' They left the room and came back with a broad smile, 'In our family, you will be called Radha — Gopal's consort.' She smiled back (I used to call her 'J' — just 'J' — the alphabet she had picked for her name when we met). J looked at me and gave a thumbs up.

'All good... I like Radha, for now. She and that Krishna dude were never married, right? She was like, a permanent girlfriend? Older? Married? Perfect!' It was my cue to break it to my parents that 'J' was five years older and had been previously married.

They were gracious enough not to react right away. My mother's smile was strained and I could recognise her old expression from my childhood — when Appa said something critical in the presence of his battleaxe mother — the formidable 'Amma' of our house. My mother was demoted to 'Akka' (sister), even for me, her only son. I used to feel sorry for Akka. She was my Amma, but I could not address her like that. My father was too terrified of his Amma. He said such feelings were common in his family where women were more domineering and controlled everything.

I was not sure what 'J' would do next. She had laughed uproariously when I had told her about meeting my folks. I could see her bright, wide-open eyes surveying our neat but modest home, taking in the protective plastic covers on the sofas and the plastic doilies on the dining table. Amma liked to cover everything in plastic. Even the table fan. I had asked,

'How can we get air from the fan when it is covered in plasic?' Amma had glared and Akka had kicked me under the table. I watched 'J' warily as she strolled around the drawing room, like she was taking an inventory. I knew she had noticed all the plastic coverings and would mention them later.

'J' went to Appa's bookshelf and picked out a hefty volume — studied the spine of Mein Kampf and put it away. 'Germans!' she said scornfully. Appa looked on — his eyes expressionless. After the traditional tea service and eating a spoonful of payasam to mark the auspicious occasion, 'J' and I left for our B-School campus on her Royal Enfield. My parents came to the gate to wave to us — which was very sweet of them.

Six years after that fateful meeting, there we were, 'J' and I, spending the lockdown period in my parent's home. We were stuck! We had nowhere else to go... as research scholars, we had to vacate our campus accommodation and leave hastily when the date was announced by the Prime Minister. We were the last to leave. We enjoyed our campus life together, smoked a lot of weed, watched strange movies — mainly those made by obscure European or Korean directors — and felt very good about ourselves. We had escaped the middle class, mediocre, predictable roots which could so easily have been our destiny. Here we were — two amazing young people sharing amazing ideals and living on our own terms. How did we know a crazy virus was about to turn our world upside down?

Akka had taken me aside on the first day itself — hours after we had flung our backpacks on what used to be my old bed —

large and comfortable, despite the lumpy mattress. She had told me firmly but also softly, that we would have to 'adjust'. Now 'adjust' was a word both of us hated. We felt we were too good to have to 'adjust' for anyone .

Akka looked at me and said evenly, 'Covid... Covid... danger.' She asked searching questions about our personal habits, which were embarrassing, and had nothing to do with Covid. She also said Amma was 'too old' and fell into the 'danger zone'. We should avoid interacting with her. 'Remember, she has diabetes and high blood pressure. She could die in two minutes if she gets the virus.' For a moment I thought there was a hopeful note in my mother's voice.

Akka leaned forward and whispered, 'Radha has been sneezing... she is not positive, na?'

I scoffed, 'What a thing to say, Akka. It's your rasam masala that is irritating her nostrils. Mine, too.'

Akka made her sarcastic face and said, 'Oh... now my boy's nostrils have also become sensitive to our rasam? Next you will say you hate curd-rice. Rasam was like mother's milk to you... now suddenly the aroma bothers you?' I calmed her down, but just then, 'J' emerged from my old room wearing cut-off shorts and her favourite ganji.

Akka's eyebrows shot up, 'If Amma sees her like this... no, no, please wear decent clothes here... we are all decent type people.' 'J' ignored her completely and asked me for a cigarette.

Akka covered both her ears and left the room. I told 'J' we would both have to... before I could complete the sentence she said, 'Adjust?'

She lit up, 'Just sit down and listen to me. Look — you and I didn't invent or unleash Covid-19 on the world. We are not guilty. Nor are we responsible. We are forced to live here because there is no other choice. It's a temp thing, yaar. Tell them to chill... can't suddenly behave all goody goody... If we feel like a doob, we should enjoy one.'

So we both lit one. Suddenly, the familiar rasam aroma surrounded us in a cloud of spices. My appetite raged... so did hers. Our Lockdown Baby project was launched that night. We just knew it had happened and joked our baby would arrive nine months later smelling of rasam and weed. And we would not name her corona. We would drink gallons of it, instead. Good for breast milk production, our friends had once told us... as if we didn't know!

NO LOVE LOST

Frankly, I didn't want to talk to anybody while strolling in my building compound during the lockdown. This was not the time to make new friends. If I had wanted to, I could have been the most popular woman in the neighbourhood. Everyone knew who I was. My television serials from the 90's were still being watched. And since no new serials were getting made in studios, people were sitting at home, makkhi maaroing and watching all these stale, flop shows.

Mind you, my roles were all very glamourous and nobody forgot how well I had played the 'saas' role in Ekta's hit show. Still, for so many years I had lived in the same building and not really mixed with my neighbours, if you know what I mean. I had zero in common with these people — they were chhota mota businessmen running shops and dukaans in arcades. Selling rubbish — China ka samaan. Now they were denying they had all that unsold Chinese maal in the store room. Just because the coronavirus came from China — no denying that fact! I agree with what that Trump chap kept saying from the beginning — corona came from China.

Bas, baat khatam. So what? Admit it, bhai? These men should not deny all their stuff is cheap made-in-China nonsense that doesn't last for a week. Why act like you are a Tata or a Birla? Am I pretending I am Mrs. Ambani? I know who and what I am. But at least I made a name for myself... earned well, saved well. I don't need anything from anybody. I am a single lady... thank God, no family! Or people would have come and sat on my head saying, 'You may die of corona... so give us all your money!'

It is my hard earned money — why should I give it to some faltu people claiming to be my rishtedar? Since when, bhai? Where were you when I had an accident on the sets and was in hospital for three months? Anyway, that's an old story. Today, I can walk with my head held high, even in this stupid building filled with stupid people, with irritating children who call me, 'Woh TV-wali aunty.' Arrey... Get lost! Aunty tere baap ki hogi. Leave me alone.

Had it not been for the lockdown, my life would have continued as nicely as always. Now, my doctor told me to go and walk downstairs or else I would again have my old problem and fall sick. He said exercise is good for me, and a little fresh air, also. I started walking even though I felt he was wrong in asking me to expose myself to infection, mixing with all those unhealthy people — maybe they had gone to China to buy all those kachrapatti things? Who knows which person was infected? These people are expert liars. They won't go for testing themselves, and they will shamelessly infect others. Besharams!

I watch news and all that – I know that at my age (not saying exact age, but you can guess), I can easily pick up the virus and if I pick it up, then toh, death is certain. Nobody recovers at this age. I am not scared of dying or anything. But why of corona? So, when neighbours offer food, snacks and all that, I refuse. They think I am being rude. But they should also realise it is not safe for me to eat their food! Who knows the state of their kitchen? What oil they use? Whether anybody has sneezed directly on the food? Do they wash their hands properly like they show on TV? I doubt it. Still... I refuse politely because I don't want to insult anybody.

Yesterday, that silly security guard called me 'Maaji'. Do I look that old? Yes, these days I cover my head with a dupatta or a scarf, because Doris, my regular salon girl, is not there to come over and give me a proper hair touch up. Mind you, I spend on good hair colour and refuse to use mehendi. I may have to change Doris – she is Chinese. And these building people won't let her enter, even after this lockdown. This is most unfair. I can also say, throw away all those Chinese goods, we are scared to get the virus which we know has come from China. But nobody is saying that! Till Doris or some other girl can come to fix my hair colour, I have to cover my head. It is bad for my fans, and my image, to be seen with white hair. I cannot recognise my own self! Such a buddhi, I suddenly look! By god – greying is not for me.

I have realised how cruel and budtameez most people are – neighbours are the worst. I may be old, but I am not deaf. I can overhear them talking in the common passage leading to the small lobby (our building is over 30 years old).

They say things like, 'If something happens to this buddhi during the lockdown... like, if she gets corona or something, how will anybody know? Who will take care of her? She has nobody. People like her should live in old people's homes and not in a decent co-operative housing society. It is not our problem if she falls sick. But if something happens to her, our building will get sealed. It will be called contaminated, and our property price will go down. All those municipalitywallas will arrive and start harassing us for nothing. No hospital will take her. Waisey bhi, there is such a shortage of ambulances and doctors. I wanted to shout, 'You bloody gadhey... look after your own bloody selves. Don't worry about me. I am taking turmeric water thrice a day and gargling with salt.'

They called this society 'decent'. Do they know the meaning of that word? At least, the old security guard who lives under the staircase gives me more izzat. He salutes me and says, 'Good evening, madam.' It feels nice to be called 'madam' again. I feel I am back in the Film City studio which had become my second home, when I was shooting for 'Ghar ki Baat' – India's craze at that time. I tip him from time to time, but if you ask me his name – sorry! I have never asked.

One young neighbour called Sapna is also good to me. She's quite considerate, unlike most young people, who lack tameez.

She offers to get me fruits and vegetables, when those vans arrive outside our compound. She says she is part of some 'buddy' system. Of course, I pay her the exact amount when she drops off three mangoes and four oranges (everyone says oranges build immunity, since they contain Vitamin C — I say, what rubbish! One will need to drink a tanker of orange juice for that to work).

Still, Sapna at least offers! Maybe she has her own matlab. Once she asked me, 'Auntyji, you must have kept up with your old contacts in television, na?' I quickly told her I had broken off from that world long ago. Then she said she wanted to audition for some dance show, because she thinks her dancing is better than Madhuri Dixit's. I just smiled and kept quiet. As if it is so easy to become Madhuri Dixit! All these thoughts come to me when I walk round and round, round and round inside our small compound. For me, keeping social distance comes naturally. I keep it anyway — lockdown or no lockdown.

Today I opened my old 'television trunk' as I call it. It is filled with all sorts of ajeeb cheez — caps and beads and high heel shoes. I found two smart caps. Good! I can wear those during my walks, so that my grey hair remains hidden. I also found large, tinted goggles, which look better than my old spectacles. I broke one arm of my chasma the other day and fixed it with a safety pin. I cannot go for a walk wearing that.

I must say, the security guard is very observant. He commented, 'Madam, as soon as the lockdown is lifted, I will come with you to the chasmawala dukaan.' I gave him ten rupees. At least, he had noticed! When he came to the flat with the electricity bill, he noticed other things also — the floors had not been swept or swabbed for a month. My unwashed clothes were lying on the armchair. There was a thick layer of dust over everything. I saw his eyes go to my small dressing table where I kept my lipstick, kaajal, deodorant, tissues. My gold bangles and diamond rings were also there, next to the cold cream jar. He definitely saw all that.

He looked around and said, 'Madam, if you want I can come and clean… once my duty hours are over.' I politely refused because, frankly, I was worried. God knows about his hygiene levels! He could also rob me under the pretext of helping me. I don't trust anybody. Whether or not he washes his hands as top filmstars show us on television. And his clothes are from his home in the nearby slums, not that he has new uniforms. Those clothes may be carrying the virus… I don't believe what I read about the virus not surviving on clothes for so many days. Why take the risk? And if he is after my bangles and rings, then he would make a plan to kill me. These people had turned desperate during corona. Our building staff had not been paid for two months. Robbing me would solve this man's problem quickly.

Last evening I met those two gossipy ladies from the tenth floor, and they were walking without maintaining a proper distance. One of them had also removed her mask from her face. So I asked loudly, 'Is the mask meant for the neck or for covering your nose and mouth? Remember, there are senior citizens living in the complex.'

Both the women glared at me angrily and that woman not obeying rules said, 'Auntyji… please mind your own business, theek hai? We know our responsibility. You keep your dialogues to yourself! Life is not a daily soap.'

I walked on, my head held high. What third class people live here. I don't feel like calling them 'padosis'. Once this lockdown business ends, I will stop my walks. And look for a replacement for Doris.

MY GIRLFRIEND'S THEPLAS

'Hey guys… let's all stay positive, okay? Bad shit happens all the time. But we can't let it kill us, na? We have to spread love… the earth is healing… I can actually see Malabar Hill from my window these days… it's so cool! And now that I have my new personalised face shields and masks and those proper imported gloves, we can really, really go all out and help — you know? I have been making theplas and rotis for the past few weeks. Not making them myself! Obviously! But helping and supervising the staff, while Mom supervises us — she hates waste! We have packed so many cartons for that NGO… I forget the name. At least we feel confident it is going to the right people — those Gandhi Nagar people.

'Haan haan… all our chhuta kaamwalas come from there only. But ever since the lockdown, they are not allowed to enter our building. I tried to argue with some show-off residents who are on the committee of my Society, that it's most awful and unfair not to allow these poor people to earn a living… come on, ya! Be honest — when was the last time you washed and scrubbed the loo yourself and removed the doggy's poop from the carpet?'

This was my dear gf talking, not me, okay?

That's Aarti for you — an enthusiastic bunny! She uses the word 'like' a lot... the same way Kylie Jenner and all use it. So, when she says, 'Like... guys! We should all like do something for charity, na?' she sounds so cute! She's a sweet, well-meaning kid. But a little confused... like, she really thought if all of us stood in our balconies beating thaalis and lighting diyas, the coronavirus would go away. Vanish!

I felt really stupid doing that monkey stuff and sending her 'proof' I had shown my patriotism and obeyed Modi by sharing selfies! God! I felt like a total loser! Problem is, she doesn't read anything beyond celebrity posts — she takes all her cues from what those famous people are saying. If Deepika and Ranveer are lighting candles on their patio and cheering frontline workers, then we must do it, too! Worst of all — she believes everything she reads on social media, and actually admires Kylie Jenner. Why am I with her if I think she's this dumb? Because... I think I love her!

We have been in a relationship for two years. Out of which I was away in Shanghai on dad's business for four months and she was vacationing in Tuscany for two. Add the lockdown period and in reality, we have been together, off and on, and in between travels, for just a little over 12 months! Dude! That's a record for me, okay? I am quite a swine... sorry to say. But not with Aarti. She is somehow... let me find the right word — yes, Aarti is pure. Not like other girls in our circle. But not meeting for all this time has been hard! I definitely miss having sex with her. She says she feels exactly the same. I know once all this ends, we will be back to our old, chilled life... nice!

Aarti is naïve and trusting, which is why I like her. She wants to be kind to anybody and everybody — humans, dogs, cats, even mice and snakes! No kidding. I told her, 'Babe, so long as you aren't kind to cockroaches and allow me to stamp on them with my heaviest boots, go ahead and be kind to all the other species in the world.' She laughed sweetly, and stuck her sharp, pink tongue into my ear.

Aarti is like a kid who I know will never grow up. But this lockdown break has given her a purpose in life. She feels important and wanted by her building buddies, who are all on a heavy-duty 'seva' mission. Nothing wrong with that — they are using their time well and helping so many people who need food, which is hygienic and properly cooked. She had put up pictures of what the government had been distributing to those migrants. Even our pets would reject that foul stuff — stale and full of fungus. Aarti is a very sincere and committed girl, in spite of all her privileges. I mean, Arti does not know the meaning of 'less', okay? She is not exactly spoilt, but, she has never taken an Ola, or used public transport.

Yes, for a while she was sounding quite silly when she wanted to go to South America and work in the slums of Rio. So many of our friends had done it, so naturally Aarti was keen to experience what it felt like to actually go slumming and live there, with the poorest of the poor. I told her, 'Baby, Brazil is not India... and you aren't going on a Copacabana beach vacation. If you want to work in Brazilian slums, first do a trial run in that Gandhi Nagar near your home.'

Suddenly, I found Aarti working feverishly in her kitchen and feeling particularly virtuous. At first I mocked her efforts and asked when she would send me her version of sourdough bread. Aarti was not amused. Distributing theplas had become a big thing in Arti's girl gang. Theplas were the thing to discuss on our friends' chat groups. Aarti was the leader of the thepla brigade and very proud of her role in motivating others to 'give till it hurts'. I encouraged her to do all this. I wanted her to wake up feeling there was some purpose to life. We both agreed it was a far better way to spend the unending lockdown time rolling out theplas (with and without methi), rather than bitching out this one and that one till 3 a.m.

Besides, Aarti was getting a lot of recognition for her thepla initiative. She had already been featured in several society columns and done interviews with prominent bloggers. She was fast becoming a Lockdown Star in her own right, participating in webinars and Insta Lives... and hold your breath — being described as a motivational speaker! Her page views had gone up — and how! Especially after she posted a cute video of hers, rolling out theplas in the kitchen, wearing a bikini top and cut off denims. I agree Aarti has a damn cute butt, and her personal maid had shot the video very nicely, with Aarti pretending to be the Thepla Queen. Her irritating pooch, the very, very yappy and thoroughly spoilt Pom called 'Doodles' (mutual hate society) also featured in the video, and suddenly Aarti was getting the sort of attention reserved for say, a Kiara or a Kriti. Totally nuts! All because of the theplas!

Aarti giggled and told me she was getting 'soooooooo many proposals', she could barely keep up! I was happy for her. Nobody used to take Aarti seriously in our group. She was called flaky and ditzy and I was teased for being the boyfriend of a 'dumb blonde'. Aarti's hair was blond, I admit. And you could call her dumb, too. But the theplas had become a game changer — she was seen as a potential youth leader, a model citizen, a girl with a heart of gold! My silly little Aarti was going places with those dumb theplas.

After the bloody thepla thing took off, Aarti felt confident enough to try and step up her other efforts. She mobilised 20 volunteers and set up help lines for senior citizens who had nobody to talk to during the long, lonely hours being stuck at home. She started taking calls herself, and her cheerful voice, silly jokes, combined with soothing words, made her so popular on her helpline, regulars would ask for her by name. She extended and expanded the basic concept to rope in therapists and counsellors who specialised in old-age related anxiety issues. She was stunned by the response! Soon, she was addressing Rotary Clubs over Zoom and talking about what we, as a society, needed to do to make our elderly feel more valued. Moved by Aarti's earnestness, a couple of top industrialists who wanted to support her initiatives contacted her. Arti roped in her building friend to create a logo for her group which she called 'Aarti Cares'.

Money and help started trickling in. The Mumbai Police called up Aarti to help out with an online appeal — they told her that cases of abuse against the elderly had gone up drastically during the lockdown, and they wanted her on board to generate awareness and launch a helpline. Aarti came up with a catchy slogan and a clever idea for a video. She requested her girl gang to shoot their grandparents as they went about their daily routines. She asked for candid footage, ideally shot in natural light. A talented musician from Aarti's class in school composed an emotional song with poignant lyrics which Aarti got another school buddy, who was now a popular tiktok star, to sing against a stark black backdrop. Together with her small team of graphic designers, she put together a lovely black and white clip, which went viral after the Mumbai Police posted it on Twitter. I watched it with my Naanaji and Naaniji who lived with us, and they were most impressed! 'Same girl?' Naaniji asked in utter disbelief. 'Same,' I answered smugly.

Soon after that, Aarti was contacted by an international women's organisation, which wanted her to be the face of a global lockdown campaign highlighting the plight of the elderly isolating themselves at home and dealing bravely with the Covid challenge, without giving up hope. This led Aarti to raise funds for adult diapers for senior citizens too weak to go unassisted to the loo on time. While others raised money for PPE suits and surgical masks for frontline workers, Aarti focused on providing sanitary napkins and adult diapers to underprivileged Covid patients in public hospitals. Within a fortnight, her loyal band of volunteers had managed to source and distribute hundreds of cartons across Mumbai.

I hardly get to connect with Aarti these days. I honestly miss her and our convos. The daily goss. She is like a woman possessed — totally consumed with work and brimming with constructive ideas for the future. Judging by her pics, her blond highlights have grown out almost completely. She is looking lovely. Of course, we still manage to chat off and on, when she can grab a few rushed minutes between her 'duties' and 'deadlines'. But I meet her more often on her Insta Feed, where she posts pictures of all the good work done by her hard working team — she now has 250 volunteers, who work from home in shifts and handle several responsibilities. Aarti has hired a coordinator to manage the work load and look at future expansion. Sarla Aunty, her efficient mother, has found a focus finally, as the two of them work seamlessly together, always side by side, making sure all the initiatives remain on a growth path. Oh — her videos have changed dramatically! Aarti no longer wears ganjis, bra tops or cut offs in the kitchen! She is always dressed in those fab india type cotton salwar kameezes — the kind she used to make fun of and call 'auntyji outfits'. She still looks pretty cute and hot — at least to me! And she boasts that the number of proposals has also gone up and up and up! Good for Aarti.

And to think it all started with theplas!

ANGIE'S BENARASI SAREE

People think I have gone mad... and that I have always been mad. They may be right. Why? Because when I tell them 'My loom talks to me' they laugh and don't believe me! But it does. It has always talked to me, from the time my grandfather asked me to sit by his side and showed me what he was weaving for a 'dulhan'. I was six or seven years old at the time. I was totally mesmerised... I practically fell into a trance. As if I was seeing a divine vision. I could not take my eyes off my Abbaji's fingers as they deftly moved and moved and moved, on that ancient, wooden loom, which had been in the family for five generations.

I silently watched my father, crouched over his own loom in another corner of the room. He was muttering his prayers softly... but the music I heard was coming from my grandfather's loom. Only I could hear it... I still hear it. And yes — my loom speaks to me. This is Abbaji's loom — he left it to me and not to my father. He understood the language of the looms. So do I.

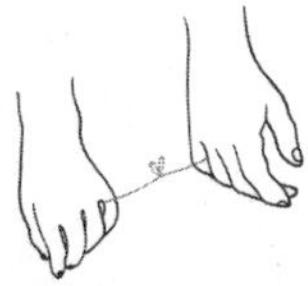

For my father, weaving was just a job. A family tradition. For me — weaving was life! Normally, my loom and I would have been communicating very happily at this time of the year. The busiest time — with order books full and buyers pestering us to deliver on time. The entire gully would have hummed with activity, with the clackety-clack of the spindles moving rapidly to weave those heavenly, hand-woven silk sarees as if only certain families from Benaras (I still call it by its original name — somehow Varanasi doesn't have the same poetry in it), had Allah's blessings.

Some of these designs were hundreds of years old. I was possessive about a few especially created by my Abbaji, and refused to share them with junior weavers. This was our family's legacy. I guarded our jaal kaam with my life. All those intricate patterns, hand drawn by skilled craftsmen over 70 years ago. My father had retired a few years ago, unable to sit crouched up in that awkward position for hours and hours. His back troubled him too much these days. So it was left to me to carry forward our family's ancient weaving traditions. I had great hopes for my son, Ali.

I wanted him to take over the pedi from me and train young weavers as I had been doing. But Ali had other plans. He wanted to become a big shot. A suit-bootwala. Get out of this locality, which is right behind the ghats, and move into the newly developed, chakachak areas of Benaras in the far end of the town. He was ashamed of our small home, and did not invite his friends over — not even during Eid.

Well... this year's Eid had been like no other Eid in my memory. In my lifetime, I hope I will never spend such an Eid. My loom was silent and sad. So was I. Our entire mohalla was silent — had been silent for two months now, after all our orders got cancelled, and the money owed to us by those who had already taken our sarees and lehengas, was not given by the middlemen. They had simply thrown up their hands and said there was none to give.

Everything collapsed overnight. Thank God I had some cash in the tin box — an advance given by a tourist — a memsaab from phoren. Imagine, this mem wanted to get married in America wearing my saree! I had sold many of my weaves to these goralog in the past, when they came to Benaras as tourists and were brought to our mohalla by guides to show how we worked. But this order was different. Her name, she told me, was Angelina — she wrote it down. But I found it hard to pronounce, so she said, 'Just call me Angie'. That was easy.

I called her 'Madam Angie', and she laughed, saying, 'No madam. Just Angie!' Such a big memsaab and so humble. She had a special request — she told me the other weavers in the gully had refused to take her order as they didn't want to deal with extra double-double work. They'd told her — 'Go to Azarbhai — he is mad! He may do it for you.'

That's how Angie came to me and asked, 'Will you weave a special saree which has my love story in it? I will pay extra for the trouble.' I immediately liked the idea, and asked my loom. Both of us agreed it was unique and a challenge we could meet if we worked very hard. She wanted it for her wedding in June. She told me it was a good time to get married in New York because the weather was always very fine at that time. We negotiated a price — I was most reasonable. I also offered her jalebis and special milk tea, which she enjoyed.

Only after that she told me her love story, which touched my heart so much, I started getting many beautiful ideas and images for this special saree. Madam Angie wanted the Taj Mahal to be a part of the design, because she had sat on the bench in front of our Taj, with the man she loved and was going to marry. Mohabbat is like that only.

But I told her, 'No madam. Please listen to this poor weaver and do not wear a mausoleum design on your wedding day. It is such an auspicious occasion. We will weave only auspicious motifs for you.'

Fortunately, she listened to me, and we decided on four or five motifs that had meaning in her life. Since her groom also loved India and had proposed to Madam Angie in Benaras, that too on the ghats, just after they had participated in the Ganga Aarti, I told her I would weave the ghat itself on the border, along with diyas, and then add whatever else she wanted to the pallu. She agreed to peacocks dancing since there were many peacocks in the garden of the hotel where both of them had stayed.

Slowly, carefully, an emotional story was created and a fresh amount fixed. I didn't overcharge her, though I could have, since this saree required months of hard work. But my loom and I were already hearing the shehnai! I started weaving Madam Angie's saree after seeking Allah's blessings and offering dua to her and her future husband, Mark Saab. After she left, we kept in touch over WhatsApp, with me using Ali's smart phone, and sending her pictures as the saree progressed on the loom.

Throughout that period, I only listened to Ustad Bismillah Khan saab playing the shehnai as only he could. I feel a weaver's mood and state of mind affects what he creates. This was a very precious responsibility given to me by a good woman. I wanted her saree to be a masterpiece! Nothing less.

While I was halfway through it, something terrible befell the world. At first, I ignored what I was hearing, and continued to weave. I told myself, these are just stories. In India, we are used to all kinds of diseases. In Benaras life and death have always co-existed through centuries — we take both for granted. I had grown up seeing funeral pyres and corpses burning on the ghats all day and all night. Death did not frighten me. But what Ali was sharing with his friends and sometimes with his ammi and me, was something far worse — it was an unknown harbinger of death and suffering. Maybe he did not want to scare us by discussing this topic. But from the little I could make out from what they were showing on television, I knew it was a major calamity... and the whole world was getting infected by... some said an insect, some said a bat, some said a chemical. But all said it came out of China.

Finally all those badey badey scientists decided it was a bat that had done this to our duniya. A bat! Tauba! Tauba! Now, this chamagaadad pakshi was known to all — we had so many in the fruit trees of Benaras. How could these pakshis kill thousands and millions of people? There must have been some mistake. I kept weaving and ignoring all those TVwallas shouting and shouting, trying to scare everybody for nothing. This carried on… till one day, I think it was March 24th, just before we sat for dinner, that I saw Modiji on the TV screen.

As you know, Benaras is very proud of the Prime Minister — this is where he fought his election and won his seat. I had personally campaigned for him! I don't feel ashamed to say it even now, unlike some others from the mohalla who are very upset and hate him. Not me! Anyway, what he said made me go numb with shock. Initially, I could not understand that within four hours our world would turn ulta-pulta and completely change! And change so fast, we would be left in this pathetic condition wondering where our next meal will come from.

I asked Ali to explain and he raised his voice. His Ammi told him to show respect and keep quiet, but Ali was angrier than I had ever seen him. He told both of us, 'I should have left this mulk two years ago and gone to New Zealand. I stayed back for what — this?' Even at that point, I didn't know the full story of the 'lockdown' — I had just learnt a new word, without understanding its place in my life. Today, I know! And my loom also knows. We console each other these days and pray for better tomorrows.

For the first time in our lives, there were no new clothes for Eid. But at least we were more fortunate than many others — we had a roof over our heads. And the money given by Madam Angie as an advance. But where had Madam Angie disappeared? I had asked Ali to contact her a few times to request her to send a little more money, since there were zero orders this year for Diwali — generally our busiest period. Ali said he had tried and received no response. Maybe Madam Angie was busy with other wedding preparations. I told him to keep trying, and not feel shy to ask for a little help. Americans are ameer and generous. She would understand and send what she could — I was very confident.

After two or three weeks of sending her WhatsApp messages and not getting a response, I began to worry. By now, I had watched on TV what was happening in New York. That big city was looking like a big kabarsthan! More bodies lying there than on our Benaras ghats. It gave me a big, big shock. The loom also felt something was wrong. It was not like Madam Angie to ignore so many messages. Only a little work remained on her saree — I had matched the blue of her shining eyes by getting the silk dyed to the exact shade before I started with the zari patterns. I had attached colourful silk tassels to the end of the pallu — those were my artistic gift to Madam Angie and not included in the original design or cost.

Her wedding date was approaching, and I was worried whether we would be able to courier the saree well in time. It was already late — and the courier services had still to resume properly. I told Ali this morning, 'Beta... try one more time.

Madam Angie ke saat baat hi karlein... she will be happy to hear my voice. Tell her we are waiting for the courier services to start. Bas! Hamarey taraf se tayyari poori hai.'

Reluctantly, very reluctantly, Ali tried. He was shaking his head while trying. As if he knew something which I didn't. Finally, in a low voice he said, 'Abba... leave it. I think... I think... no, I really can't say... I don't know anything... but her number has been dead for two weeks now. I didn't want to tell you... maybe Madam Angie ...'

I held up my hand, and said sharply, 'Stop!'

I no longer listen to the shehnai. My ears have changed, so has my heart. As for my stomach? It has shrunk to half its size – how can I fill it, when my loom is equally hungry? We sit in this room all day, waiting for someone and something, consoling each other. I have stopped listening to the shehnai since that day when Ali tried to contact... No, I cannot even get myself to utter her name. The saree with the love story is packed away in a trunk. No other dulhan can ever wear it. The loom and I only listen to the silence of the ghats these days.

VODKA... AND NO TONIC

I hate this lockdown nonsense, okay? As it is we were having problems in our marriage — his work, my work... usual story. Then came this bloody, fucking lockdown! And after 20 days, I was ready to die of coronavirus rather than spend one more day and night with this awful man. The thing is, I did not know he was awful! Till the lockdown happened. In fact, I thought I had married a nice chappie.

We knew each other from before getting hitched and all that. Not as if one fine day our parents came up with a rishta and we said 'yes'. Nor was it one of those bakwas dating sites... or an NRI type of kahani. We lived in the same colony! We were both fauji bachchas. We understood each other's lifestyles. Our schooling was similar. We worked hard, you know? Did MBA and all that — separately, of course. So hard work was not some new concept — arrey, we were not Ambanis, Birlas and Tatas. Solid middle class values! But we had big dreams — why lie? We wanted to make it big in the world. Travel from Tokyo to Paris. Do fun stuff together. Set up an amazing home. Paartyshaarty with friends – typical.

Our wedding was too much fun, yaar. All the events put together by a wedding planner so nicely – just the other day, I was watching the videos on my laptop and thinking, 'Yaar... look at these! How happy we look! And I toh looked super hot, especially during the bikini shoot in Phuket, where we went with four other couples for our youngsters' party.

Watching those videos during the lockdown added to my depression. It was all past tense. Our lives had changed forever. And I knew, no matter how hard we both tried, our marriage would never be the same again. Vicky has changed – that much is pucca. He says I have changed – lies! I am still the same Manju – ask my friends! We chat and have Zoom parties every other evening – just to remind ourselves we are alive. Vicky finds all this stupid and refuses to join us. He locks himself in the bedroom and creates a racket, just to disturb my fun. Of course, I drink during these virtual parties. Why not, yaar! It's not a crime! What else does he expect me to do! Japamala?

Just because he has zero friends, he is jealous of mine. I am friendly and sociable, okay? He also used to be like that. We had common friends. Then he slowly changed – which he denies. How can he deny this? Why blame everything on the lockdown? I told him not to give me excuses and keep running away from the real issues. The truth is, we no longer sleep together. I admit it was my decision to give sex a break – it was getting too much for me! I worked in Gurugram, and he in Noida. We were both doing brilliantly – the money and perks were good. But the hours were long, and we both had to travel a lot. Naturally, this would lead to fatigue — all my girlfriends told me the same thing. So, my group decided to get off this whole 'sex-ka-chakkar' for a while.

'Let's detox sexually,' we said. And laughed a lot. I was relieved I wasn't the only woman sick of sex. But Vicky took it very personally. He thought I was rejecting him! I said there is a difference between rejecting sex and rejecting him. He didn't get it and stopped talking to me.

Two days after this happened, lockdown also happened. We were stuck. And my life got fucked!

Our apartment is not small, but it is not spacious-spacious either. We have a balcony and all that. Ha ha ha, the same balcony from which I feel like jumping off, these days, when things get too much. Then, I look at my plants, which I love, and say to myself, 'I can't do such a terrible thing to them! After all, what have they done? And if I die, they will also die, since Vicky will not water them.' He refuses to!

Once, when I was busy on my work call and requested him to just water them, since they looked thirsty, he flatly refused, saying rudely, 'It is not my job.' I was hurt. As if watering plants is a 'job'. Those plants are my real babies — since we don't have a baby together. And this is his reaction?

What if we had had a kid in this situation! A kid without a maid, and the two of us trying to cope. I would have definitely jumped out — with the kid. Because I know Vicky would not have helped take care of our baby either. He said watering the plants was 'not his job'. Then what is his job? I forgot to mention, he has been laid off. So, he doesn't have any other job. Maybe he is jealous that I still have mine. But that he won't admit. The house is in my name. Why? Because the loan is also in my name. Of course, we both shared the EMIs, but even then, I paid more than he did, since I earn more.

This was never a problem — till the lockdown. We used to even joke about it, and he would tell friends, 'Aren't I lucky? I am a kept man — Manju keeps us in style!'

I would think, 'Wow! Vicky is so confident, unlike other husbands. He doesn't have any ego hassles admitting I am more successful. He is so secure!' Now look at him! Growling and sulking all day. Cribbing about every little thing!

It's difficult to sleep on the same bed night after night without accidentally touching one another. I mean — bodies shift at night, na? He flips out if my hand or leg fall over any part of him. As if I am doing it on purpose. And then a whole drama follows — he angrily switches on all the lights and switches off the air-conditioner, just to spite me. Even though it is April, and it is close to 40 degrees outside.

'I am so hot!' I complained and he laughed, 'Oh really? You... and hot? Dream on!' I would have kept quiet, but I am paying the electricity bills! So I let him have it!

He picked up his phone (the latest, most expensive model I had given him for his birthday, just before the lockdown), and started to video record my outburst, saying, 'Let your WhatsApp chat groups see you like this. Then they will know why I don't want to live with you.' This was the first time he had uttered those words, without actually saying, 'Divorce'.

So, naturally I screamed, 'You coward — why can't you just say you want to divorce me?' This was exactly what he wanted to hear! I had used the 'D-Word' — not him. He was armed with 'evidence'.

He waved the phone at me triumphantly, 'Oh ho... now let the fun begin!' He thought of divorce as 'fun'? Our divorce? Had he gone totally mad?

I called my best friend Shanti — the calm and mature one from the group. She was 'just a housewife' she would say at parties, and I would kick her ankle. Her advice was simple and sensible, 'See Manju, it is because of the lockdown. People are going crazy across the world. Vicky did not mean it. He must have felt you were provoking him — all this going on in the middle of the night. You keep quiet and mind your own business. Stay out of his path. Everything will be okay after the lockdown is lifted.'

I felt better as I made coffee for myself — he had stopped drinking 'my' coffee a week or so ago. I went to my work desk and logged in. There were dozens of mails pending — the usual mid-week chaos. My mind was very disturbed, and I felt a vodka tonic would help me get through the long day.

So, I went to the cabinet to look for the bottle of Belvedere we had bought at duty free during our last trip to Bali. It was missing. What the fuck! I stormed into the bedroom and found Vicky fast asleep even though it was eleven in the morning – this had become a regular thing. I asked firmly, 'Where's the Belvedere?'

He opened one eye and laughed into my face, 'Lipstick in the morning? Pearls? Must be a special video conference – looking for a new catch already?'

I went and shook him, a little roughly, I admit, and he jumped back, 'I will call the police and report you for assaulting me.' I stood motionless and stared at the man I thought I knew so well and had once loved – yes, loved!

I composed myself and hissed, 'Just give me the bottle – now!' He grinned and said, 'What bottle? It's not your bottle. It's mine. I paid for it, remember?'

I heard myself say, 'Okay... I will pay you back in cash. Right now! Just give me the fucking bottle.'

He continued to loll in bed as he mocked me by mimicking my Haryanvi accent. He was from Himachal, and had been to a public school, briefly. I couldn't take it! I just couldn't – I knew I was being stupid, but I rushed towards him and lunged. In the bargain, I tripped over the Kashmiri bedside rug, and fell.

It was a nasty fall. No blood, no cuts, no scratches. But several bruises and a black eye. I immediately reached for my phone and took a video of myself.

I acted! I was so convincing! I sobbed and sniffled as I spoke about my husband assaulting me without the slightest provocation. I cut to images of me applying an icepack to my rapidly puffing eye, and cut to Vicky seated on a rumpled bed, looking stupefied.

Let's see what the lawyers have to say about this! I can't wait for the courts to open.

STUCK

Boss... here I am stuck inside my Delhi home. My wife and two boys are hundreds of miles away, in our family home. We live in a joint family... but we have enough independence and space for all, including my grandparents. My wife often complains it's very hard for her to deal with four generations living under one roof. See... she's a modern girl and enjoys her life. We are a tight group — you know?

Couples who work together, travel together, party together. There is a comfort level happening, because we know each other's secrets — who can sneak on whom? Everyone keeps 'chhup', but we all know who is having a scene and where. My work brings me to Delhi. In fact, most of what I do as a successful businessman involves being in Delhi. Since I used to spend at least two days of the week in Delhi, my wife and I had decided it made more sense to buy a place here — this lovely bungalow where I am staying right now. I was meant to go back home the next afternoon — and suddenly, a nationwide lockdown was announced and the borders got sealed.

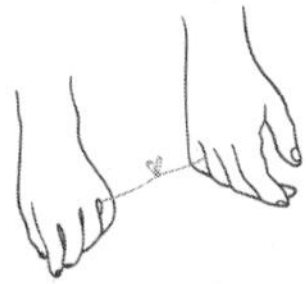

I admit my first reaction was, 'Yaaaay! I can spend time here on my own, and not have to deal with the constant "chik-chik" from my wife about who had said what to her during my absence.' I had trained myself to hear, but not hear, her non-stop grumbling. After she had finished, it would be my mother's turn to bitch out my wife, followed by my grandmother, who would attack me for being away all the time!

My boys never troubled me. I enjoyed their company, since they were teenagers now, and we could play gully cricket together. I really missed being back with them. Just them. And let me be perfectly frank — Sweety (my wife's pet name) and I had stopped having regular sex a few years ago. I mean — with each other! Hahahaha. I used to freelance during my trips abroad, and Sweety had a thing going with one of the guys from our group. I knew about their affair, but I reasoned after being married for 16 years, a woman also gets tired of daily daal-chawaal sex — she needs Thai curry. Just as I needed a full murg massalam after eating veggie meals at home.

My 'murgis' were mostly from Delhi — attractive, smart working girls. One particular corporate lawyer was my favourite — she was helping me sort out a messy contract, so naturally we spent many evenings together, going over the fine print. Sometimes, Ronita stayed over and left after breakfast. She had started keeping a change in one of the closets in the guest room.

My staff was used to my ways, and their lips were sealed.

Thank God I had employed three smart Nepali men and one driver from Bihar on a permanent basis. They lived in the servant's quarters and minded their own business. I was very good to them, so nobody could crib about anything. They were also taken aback by the lockdown but assured me I would be well looked after by them.

My problem was what to do with Ronita. She was also stuck inside my home and this was getting most awkward. What would she say to her mother in Chandigarh? Or to her seniors who had asked her to WFH? Wouldn't they wonder whose home? Her friends were cool about all this — I wasn't her first client-boyfriend, as she herself had assured me. But this situation was too much! The first few days were like an extended honeymoon — we stayed in bed all day and fucked each other's brains out. We imagined we had fallen in love, and started fantasizing about a life together once the lockdown was lifted. Stupid! As if it works like that.

Then came the reality check — I was used to Sweety doing everything for me — all my day-to-day comforts were taken care of, even in this home. She would call the staff 20 times a day to give them detailed instructions — what to cook, how to serve my meals, which clothes to keep out on the bed every morning — that way, she was the perfect wife. We never ran out of anything, and I didn't have to bother about rubbish things like toilet paper rolls and electricity bills. It was done!

The staff guys loved Sweety, because she looked after them well — sent presents for their wives in Nepal, gave old toys for their children, organised their uniforms (summer and winter — different sets). Now, with Ronita around, the staff did not know whom to obey — the madam in the house, or the missing memsaab. I didn't want to interfere, so I left it to Ronita to sort this out directly. Sorry to say, she made a complete mess. Her excuse was that she was 'freaked out' by the lockdown! Arrey... what nonsense. As if the whole world wasn't freaking! Then, she said the staff did not listen to her, and only took orders from Sweety.

But Ronita, who had never run a proper home, should have realised that she was plain lousy at it!!! She was more the barsaati type — casual. My beautiful bungalow was a mess! The staff had given up. Plus, the driver, with no work, and nowhere to drive me, was keen to go back to his village, since he didn't want to 'die alone' in Delhi! The Nepali men were also panic-stricken, and not getting it that the borders were sealed! There was nothing I could do to get them to Kathmandu.

All day, the only talk around the table was corona corona corona. I had stopped watching television completely, and had started to avoid Sweety's calls. I did not want to facetime the boys either, or engage in zoom conferences and webinars. I was looking terrible, without my weekly grooming sessions with Rashidbhai. My straggly beard and unkempt hair had aged me by ten years.

As for Ronita — dear God! Her upper lip was worse than mine. She had a proper mooch! Her eyebrows looked like caterpillars crawling across her forehead, and the rest of her was hairier and scarier than I could have visualised. Plus, she was seriously greying — ALL over! Which could only mean she had lied to me about her age. But I had also lied about mine! She was also very sloppy around the house — I was used to tidiness, thanks to Sweety's good, neat habits. Ronita liked eating her meals on the bed. When she dropped achaar on the duvet and stained it I flipped out completely! My duvet was very expensive! Imported! Sweety had sourced it from a London store that specialised in hand-crafted bed linen. Sweety would be furious! Achaar stains never go, and my staff members would definitely report this, for fear of being held responsible for the damage. I am also wondering how I have landed in this situation! She has no business to be here, but there is nothing I can do.

I tried using my Delhi police contacts to find out if I could send her back somehow. She told me her area falls in the red zone and her neighbours would not let her into the society, without a proper Covid test. I did not ask her 'Which area is that?' That was stupid of me. I am equally worried — what if she is an asymptomatic Covid 19 carrier? I don't want to die like this! I heard her sneezing and sniffling yesterday. She pretended some pepper from the pepper mill was irritating her nose. How come it did not irritate mine? We were eating our eggs together on the same table. Now she wants to smoke a sheesha every evening, saying it relaxes her... and what else can we do to keep ourselves amused, now that my liquor cabinet has been emptied and we can't score any bottles from our friendly neighbour. Poor chap, even he has finished his last bottle of Hendrick's and has opened a rare cognac he was saving up for his wedding anniversary.

I am not a sheesha fan, and it's too hot to sit outside in any case. But Ronita is one stubborn bitch! She argues too much. I told her to shove the sheesha up her butt – come on, ya! There's a limit to a guy's patience. She has also started throwing abuses around and I told her sternly to stop or else.

She laughed and asked, 'Or else... what?' I promptly shut up. My staff complained about her and said they will not listen to her instructions, after she told them to 'fuck off' because they refused to go out and get her a packet of ciggies at 10 pm. Bahadur reminded her that there was a night curfew on... and she yelled, 'Fuck the curfew... fuck everything... get me those fucking cigarettes.'

I couldn't say a thing, and I couldn't control her, either. Finally, I phoned Sweety. She was the only one who would know what to do. And she did. At first she pretended to be shocked and enraged. But I could tell from her voice that she was acting – how could Bahadur not have told her about Ronita? I started by saying, 'Sorry... Please, please, please baby... forgive me.'

I was ready to tell her everything, start to finish. But she wasn't interested and cut me short by saying, 'Shut up... idiot! Such a chhoot you are!'

I had gone to the guest bathroom to make the call. I sat on the potty and talked to Sweety using my honeymoon voice. She knew me inside out, and said sharply, 'Forget all your jalebi dialogues — let me figure out how to get rid of that randi in your bed. I hope she has not stained my beautiful linen.'

Oh God! So Sweety knew about the achaar stain! I lied and said, 'No no no... Sweety baby... don't worry. You just tell me how to get out of this bloody mess. And what to do with that bitch.'

Sweety paused, 'There is only one way out... tell the driver to pretend he is ill and you make a fake call to a doctor. Tell her you suspect the driver is positive and that the house will be sealed when that gets confirmed. Sneeze a few times in her presence and make a fake call to Dr. Aggarwal. Look worried. Summon the staff and tell them to pack a bag for you since you were certain you would have to isolate yourself one way or the other. Keep repeating strict quarantine, strict quarantine, whenever she's around. Tell the bitch she will have to get out somehow as you don't want her to die, too. Scare the shit out of her. Lie that you fall into the most vulnerable category since you are diabetic. Make it sound authentic — say diabetes runs in both sides of the family, for three generations. Tell her to move into the guest room for her own protection. Phone me openly in her presence and talk about missing the boys and all that senti stuff. She will shit bricks — trust me! And she will go running back to wherever she came from.'

Sweety was so right. Sweety is always right. Ronita fled. And I have placed an online order for an identical duvet from the same London store. It will arrive as soon as deliveries start happening. The stained duvet has been given to the driver. He has kept it carefully packed in a thick plastic cover. He said his wife in Kathmandu will need it during Nepal's harsh winters. And she won't notice or care about the achaar stain because she is not a memsaab.

DOCTOR DOCTOR

'I am tired of hearing how tired you are, okay? I am also tired. Everybody is tired. The whole world is tired.' I didn't mean to snap. But I had been through a long day myself. Looking after a Covid ward in an overcrowded public hospital is not a joke.

The worst part was the wretched PPE suit. I used to feel like a broiled lobster once I got into it. None of us had any idea how grossly uncomfortable the entire drill would become — from clambering into the suit, then those shoe covers, gloves and face masks. Once we climbed inside that space suit we couldn't really get out easily. Not even to pee! It was that cumbersome! Which meant we had to train our bladders and ignore nature's call, no matter what.

Yup. Those damn suits were that cumbersome. Some of my colleagues got UTIs because of it. I decided to be practical and switched to adult diapers. No choice! Nitin laughed and laughed when he saw the packet. I thought that was a little mean of him. It's not as if I was enjoying wearing those nappies! I had developed a rash on my private parts because of the discomfort of that scratchy diaper... he really should have been more sensitive. Did he even realise what it was like delivering babies in those wards? I hated the idea of bringing new life into this wretched Covid-19 world.

My whole thinking had changed overnight. I was sure after we had dealt with this virus, there would be another... and another... and another. Nitin found such talk morbid and told me I needed to consult our common psychiatrist friend. He made it sound like I was going nuts, when I knew it was the additional stress of hospital duty and nothing else!

Yes, even those shooting pains in my neck... stress! Common condition, I kept saying, with him asking, 'Then how come I am not showing all these weird symptoms? As if I am not dealing with stress.'

I told him we were not competing in the stress department. My stress was my stress. How would he know my threshold? It wasn't as if I was faking all this. He made it sound like I was a compulsive attention seeker, dying to focus on myself, when all of us needed to reach out and help other, more vulnerable people. I told him not to lecture me. Either he understood my position, or he didn't.

He said, 'I don't! Remember, I am also a doctor. If I don't "understand", nobody else will. Remember also, you are a highly qualified, very successful gynae, not an illiterate, unpadh village woman. You should be able to take care of all these new demands without making such a song and dance over it.' And he stupidly mentioned the names of my colleagues, saying, 'See how they are behaving! Learn from them.'

Bloody insensitive! I was so furious! Those Covid wards were worse than hell. He had been spared the ordeal. But I had been roped in, even though I was most reluctant. I had tried to make some excuse and get out of reporting for duty. This was just not fair! So much pressure on doctors, as if they were not ordinary human beings, also worried about their own health. I didn't want to die of Covid!

And how much precaution could I take, in any case? My husband was behaving like an unpadh himself and insisting large, imported tablets of Vitamin C swallowed three times a day, would make us both totally immune to picking up the virus. Next he would tell me to swallow what that ass Trump was swallowing and recommending.

I had said nicely, 'Please watch those reports and briefings on CNN — there is no cure for Covid! Even if a vaccine is found tomorrow morning, we still won't get it at a pharmacy for two more years. Stop behaving like our foolish neighbours! They aren't doctors — we are!' That Mrs. Gupta keeps sending me Whatsapp messages about drinking three gallons of hot turmeric water daily and biting into soaked peppercorns.

I told her straight, 'If you think this is a preventive, why isn't the whole world taking it?' She shut up after that.

When I worked and slaved to become a doctor, I chose to become a gynae. That was then! How could I have anticipated this Covid thing hitting the world? I certainly hadn't imagined I would be sweating it out for 14–18 hours in a stinking, overcrowded hospital, delivering babies of women who had tested positive. Some were asymptomatic. Others were running fever and coughing. Frankly, nobody wanted to touch them! Even the nurses were scared. So many had left their jobs and gone back to their villages in Kerala, which meant we were hopelessly short-staffed in those wards.

Every single day, I would pull out wiggly babies from those infected wombs and go to the loo to throw up! I had started to hate the sight of full term, swollen stomachs, with inverted belly buttons and discoloured skin. The whole point of pregnancy had started to nauseate me all of a sudden. I wanted to tell these women something... shout at them... scold them. What fools! Idiots! One more hungry mouth to feed in this terrible world! Those kids would have to deal with toxic gases, polluted seas, wars and worse epidemics in the future. Was it worth it? I couldn't sleep at night, with my dark, bad thoughts. I often lay awake contemplating killing those squirming things... those newborns... strangling them with the umbilical cord and throwing them into the garbage bin. Couldn't these mothers see what they had done? I was losing it!

My husband and I had met in medical school, he was my senior. But somehow we were on the same wavelength from the very first meeting in the maternity ward, when I was the junior doctor, whose job was to go from ward to ward, checking the blood pressure of pregnant ladies and also checking their ankles for swelling. I would do the rounds enthusiastically... especially when our senior doctors turned up, along with the nursing staff.

I was living in the hostel, and this senior doctor actually noticed me in a group of five junior doctors. He singled me out, and tried to test my competence by telling me to examine a woman who was in her third trimester and experiencing discomfort... spotting. Never a good sign. I must have impressed him, as he started to ask for me by name whenever he came for his rounds. By the time I graduated, he was already a well-established 'Doctor Nitinsaab', an ENT consultant with a good practice.

We had been dating throughout those demanding years – with the approval of both families. When my mother asked anxiously, 'Is it a good idea for a doctor to marry another doctor?' Nitin beamed, put his arm around me and replied, 'The best idea! We understand the pressures and know how to cope during emergencies.'

He was right. We had the training not to allow work pressures to get to us. Nitin was well-respected in his field as the go-to ENT chap, while I had a decent reputation as a gynae. Between us, we made good money. Oh yes! Mumbai was great for well-qualified professionals like us — it was a teeming metropolis filled with very sick and very rich people.

My client base was made up of wealthy, pregnant bahus who came to see me each time they experienced a 'symptom' — such stupid things — those symptoms! Did they have zero common sense? Not that I was complaining — each time they walked in, I made three thousand rupees telling them not to worry, everything was going fine with the pregnancy.

'Dr. A', they called me, and I liked appearing cool, young, understanding and clued in with these silly, spoilt creatures. South Mumbai socialites and their pampered daughters-in-law would coo, 'Mummyji only trusts Dr. A.' They would tell everybody proudly, 'We are part of Dr. A's super exclusive baby club. My gawwwwd! Her waiting list is crazy! I'm so glad she somehow managed to fit me in, when one of her patients slipped in the jacuzzi and had a miscarriage. Yaaa... I know, so saaaad, na?'

In that sense, Nitin and I weren't competitors. Nor did our crazy hours interrupt our social life. It did not really interfere with our sex life either — you know? We managed somehow, between his appointments and mine! Coitus Interruptus? That was us! Champions at quickies. Like most docs. We had a super set of cool friends. It was understood weekends were for fun. We both avoided working on Sundays, so we could enjoy our drinks on Saturday, watch a movie, go to the club bar. It was great that things had worked out very nicely. No loans to worry about, two foreign trips, a staff of three. And best of all — two drivers. Mine and his.

Then came the news about my driver Haribhau testing positive.

I had suspected something was wrong when he complained of a headache as we were driving to the temporary Covid-19 maternity ward in the hospital for an emergency C-section. I asked if he had fever and he said 'no'. He had been staying in the garage downstairs from the time the lockdown was announced. Which was a good thing. If he had gone to his home in Andheri, he would have been stuck there and unable to report for duty. The driver network in our building was very good. Some of them decided to stay in the basement, which had two bathrooms for workers. I was so relieved when Haribhau told me he was downstairs, and I could call him up for duty anytime. I discussed it with my my husband and we decided to give him two meals, tea, coffee and biscuits, bottled water, sanitizer, soap, two towels and a deo. Better he ate clean food from our kitchen rather than what the other drivers cooked in that filthy basement. Haribhau was thankful. He asked for a small advance to be sent to his wife and mother staying in his room in the suburbs. I was a bit startled. I had no idea he had a wife and a mother! What I mean is, I had not given his personal life any thought.

Mind you, the decision to stay with other drivers in that basement had been taken by Haribhau himself. I had not asked him to stay there. He said he needed the salary and didn't want to risk losing his job once the lockdown was lifted. We were totally fine with it. Frankly, I was relieved and secretly delighted. But I didn't show it to Haribhau. Didn't want him to take advantage of the situation and ask for more money. We were not like those other horrible people who exploited servants. We had decided to pay salaries in full. We understood these are poor people. And they were not shirking duty. They were willing to drive us wherever. But there was nowhere to go! They were there 'on duty', but minus any duties. Most of our friends thought we were mad! They had not paid their staff at all! Some had reluctantly given half a month's salary. They told us, 'You are being ridiculous… do we get paid if we don't work?' In a way, they had a point.

'How can we pay for work that is not being done? You mean, we should pay for them to sit at home aaram se, doing nothing? Makkhi maroing, while we have to suffer so much inconvenience! My house plants have not been watered in weeks! How can I lift heavy buckets of water and water them?' said the wife of Nitin's golfing partner.

Another said she had cut four days' salary, since the lockdown was announced on the 24th of the month, and her daily cleaning lady had not been allowed into the building after that day. Nitin and I were not so stingy and unreasonable. Our building people were also equally generous. We all agreed it was a blessing to have at least one or two staff members with us during the lockdown. We didn't mind paying them a little extra also. I told Haribhau the same thing — 'I will pay you something more after this corona problem ends. Don't worry.' I couldn't drive. And Nitin had said clearly he wasn't going to do 'driver duty'.

My professional life had started to revolve around Haribhau. I spent more time with him than with Nitin! What would I have done without Haribhau? Good man. Loyal and silent. We hardly spoke – there was really no need for any conversation. I was always handling calls while travelling to my clinic. And I preferred it this way. Our only 'connection' took place when our eyes met in the rear view mirror, while I instructed him. Even the car keys were handed over to Haribhau every morning by our house help.

When Haribhau came down with a mild fever, I had no choice but to send him to the nearest testing centre, where he had to queue up for five hours before someone attended to him. And that was after I made a few calls to the local MLA whose wife was my patient. I told him to phone and inform his wife and mother. Frankly, it was their responsibility. Nitin was shocked when we were asked to pay five thousand rupees for the test. He told me his golfing friend mentioned that he had paid over a lakh and a half to have his daughter's maid treated at one of those new facilities. Nitin made it very clear he would not cough up in case Haribhau tested positive.

I admit, at this stage I was only thinking of myself. Not Haribhau or his family members. I was being selfish! Call me heartless, I don't care. If Haribhau tested positive, I'd be stuck in every which way! I would also have to self-quarantine. All the people I had interacted with would be traced and tested – I would be shunned. My neighbours would start hating me and those Municipal men would turn up to seal our building, put up that ugly, big sign! We would be held responsible for causing this problem, as if we had personally unleashed corona. As if we had done it deliberately. All because of Haribhau and his carelessness. He must have picked it up from one of the other drivers, even though I had explained the dangers of relaxing too much with those men in the basement. Even if he did survive — I am being brutally honest — Nitin and I would not be able to keep him.

My mind was already working on replacing Haribhau once the lockdown lifted. Good drivers were really tough to find in our city. Of course, Nitin and I would pay him a little extra and all that. And I would give his pregnant wife (Haribhau had told me his wife was pregnant on the day that he went for the Covid test) all the free tonics and samples and vitamins lying with me. But the question of keeping him did not arise. Sorry. But we have to be practical and think of ourselves also. Times are really bad.

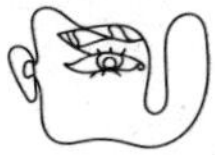

PEACE, AT LAST

I knew I had married the wrong man on the wedding night itself. My husband got it up, but he couldn't get it in! He struggled for a few seconds, pushed my body around, muttered under his breath and finally gave up. I kept mum. He didn't.

'It's your fault... the position of your legs was all wrong,' he said.

I apologised and stroked his back, 'Let's try after some time... I will adjust my legs.' My voice was soft and humble, my eyes were downcast. I had apologised for something – but what? I had apologised for nothing! But I had unwittingly given him an alibi. A face-saver. He was a lousy, inexperienced, inept, clumsy, insensitive and selfish lover.

That's the truth. I had nothing to apologise for – but I had done it. I had said 'Sorry!' How stupid of me! Just to maintain peace and not damage his ego. I didn't want my marriage to start on the wrong note. His ego. It was always about his ego.

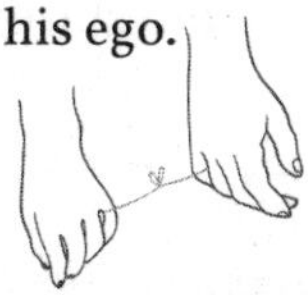

What about my ego? Was it less precious? His hurt feelings — no thought spared for mine?

So many years later, I now realise, had I saved the apology right then on our marital bed, I would have saved myself several subsequent hurts and insults. After that fateful flop of a sexual encounter, our sex life fell into a predictable groove. We had a pattern in place — if he couldn't penetrate or couldn't achieve an orgasm it was because the fault was entirely mine. Either, I did not know how to 'please' him, he said, or my body was 'of the wrong shape'. Had he not seen his own shape?

Sex is the key to marriage. Good sex keeps a marriage going. Bad sex kills it. When sex stops — the marriage ends. I know when my marriage ended. It was the day I decided to end sex with my husband once and for all. Not because sexual desire had left me. But because I was finally strong enough to say 'no' to my husband's unreasonable and far-too-frequent sexual advances. I felt my 'duty' was over. We had three children, who looked just like him. So, the world would know our marriage had been 'normal'. No fooling around! Paternity well established and stamped all over the children.

But now, I had made up my mind that enough was enough. My body was my own. And I could no longer oblige my husband sexually. This decision was taken a good ten years after menopause. Ten long years during which I did not protest or resist, even though my hormones were rebelling and my heart hurt. I tried. I didn't want him to lose interest in me and start looking for sex outside the home. We were set in the standard comfort zone of most middle class marriages. Enough food. Zero sex.

So, for ten long years, I would automatically part my legs and let him in — even though my vagina was dry, and I was in pain. He would curse under his breath if he couldn't penetrate me as easily as in the past. I would stifle my cries somehow. But I couldn't stop my tears. My entire being was in revolt. Not just my body. I started dreading the night — the thought of sleeping next to him. I would light a diya at sundown and pray to God to spare me the torture.

'Please... let him be too tired. I beg you, dear God, make him leave me alone. I need to sleep. I am fatigued. I am sick of pleasing him! It hurts!' I tried telling him how menopause affects a woman. How her hormones change. How her vaginal muscles lose elasticity. How the mucus lining can no longer release sufficient secretions to keep the passage smooth and moist. But he'd be too busy roughly thrusting. I don't think he heard me. Or if he did, he didn't really care. For, he didn't stop.

Not that day, not the next day... not for the next decade. His body repulsed me. His breath made me want to push his face away. I had stopped kissing him much earlier, but just the proximity of his mouth so close to mine, as he grunted and heaved, would make me want to throw up. I would hold my breath, shut my eyes tight, my arms would lie lifelessly, or I would tuck my hands under my buttocks, so as not to embrace him.

He noticed nothing! He didn't sense my rejection, as he pinched my nipples, and cupped my breasts. I refused to look into his eyes — the same eyes that ravaged my body even when I was fully clothed. How could he not feel terrible, and small and diminished and...? Did nothing matter but those few seconds of penetration? The 'union' as he called it? Did he really believe all that nonsense about 'feeling as one' or 'feeling complete' when he had forced entry into me? What about my emotions? My responses, as he clumsily climbed on top of me? How could he have been oblivious to my loathing? Was he that thick-skinned? Or that selfish, he simply did not care?

I didn't matter. My contempt didn't matter. My lack of interest didn't matter. So long as he could release his sperm freely inside me — freely and confidently. No chance of pregnancy at my age! So forget the condom. The condom he had always hated to wear. Now, it wasn't required! Let him drip away... down my thighs, on my belly — that sticky, smelly, viscous fluid I would hastily rub off — with tissues, with a hand towel, with my discarded saree... with anything that would cleanse me.

Did he not feel bad that I reacted this way — like he had polluted me? Did he not notice me running to the bathroom the minute he was done, to wash myself clean — of him? I would stay inside, scrubbing and scrubbing myself, much after every little trace of his sperm had disappeared from my body. Often, I would weep — in rage. Feel used and cheap and violated. Would hate myself for not having the guts to tell him to go to hell. For not pushing him off me. For obediently undressing – just for him, because I was too scared to refuse. Scared of what? Would he have struck me, for refusing sex? Who knows?

He was a man prone to violent outbursts. After a couple of drinks, he could be vicious and aggressive. I didn't want to risk being hit. It was simpler and quicker to submit to his demands and get it over with. I started to keep a count of how many times he 'did it' in a week. Twice? Thrice? When did it become once a fortnight? Then once a month? And finally – the day of my release – it stopped altogether? It took him ten years for him to get the message.

Imagine! Ten years during which I felt nauseated each time he touched me. Knowing there was no love in that touch. Just lust. Or a warped idea of love. For if he had loved me, he would not have forced himself on me – no matter what. He would have been sensitive to my changed body, which could no longer accommodate his hunger. He would have felt tender and protective, when I pleaded it was difficult for me to participate in sexual bouts. When he could see I was in pain, my thigh muscles contracted, my knees reluctant to part. And yet, he would mount me with cold, calculated determination, uncaring about my resistance.

There were times when I felt murderous. Had there been a knife by the bedside, I might have plunged it into him. Anything to escape sex. Sex… something I had once enjoyed. But which had now become the worst punishment. Sex…

something I had once enjoyed. But not with him. With my first boyfriend. We were college mates and I suppose it was puppy love gone nuts. We couldn't wait to be together, grabbing any and every opportunity we could find. Thank god we had a common friend whose liberal parents looked the other way when he let us use his bedroom and sat outside reading a book till we finished our business. Those three years was when I discovered my body and all its pleasures. When did I allow sex to become the worst punishment imaginable? What a great loss! I had forgotten my body was like a sitar that could produce the most beautiful music if played right by a talented musician. The man I married was not even a talented plumber! As for music – only false, discordant notes from his side. And a besuri, off-key raag from mine.

It was during the Covid-19 lockdown crisis that our relationship collapsed completely. I was sick of pretending. I could no longer endure his demands. I was just too fatigued! I would stare at my dull eyes in the bathroom mirror. My tears had dried up, and my heart had turned to stone. This man! I must have slept with him thousands of times over the years. Thousands! But not once had I felt desired. Suddenly, here we were, dealing with something bigger than our miserable lives. And because it was so much bigger, every emotion got exaggerated. And I decided to tune out completely. While he followed each new piece of information about Covid-19 this and Covid-19 that, I slipped further and further away into my own world. And all of a sudden, I found myself in a new universe which was calm and soothing. How and when did this happen?

I think I know. It was when I started enjoying my own body and what it was capable of, when I finally let go of my inhibitions. Sexual. Emotional, mental. My energies were invested in my breath. Each breath I took, became a chance to live again. My husband had become incidental. He was merely an instrument who let me create my own music. Nobody could rob me of those symphonies. My ear pods have saved me — I swear. These days, I go about my housework, since we have no live-in staff. He watches TV all day and for half the night, while I busy myself cooking our daily meals, and keeping the house clean. I have shut out the world, the same way the world has shut me out. I am not complaining. I have never been so much at peace.

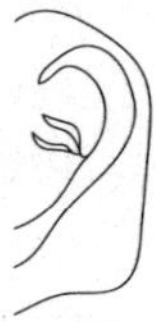

WEDDING CANCELLED

'Beta, just try one more time, na? That designer's second assistant used to be in college with you... explain to her... what use is the lehenga now? Where will you wear it?' Mummyji could be so insensitive and crude, sometimes. As it is I was feeling terrible... like, crying my eyes out. And she had to bring up the lehenga! As if the lehenga is more important than my feelings. She keeps saying Pappaji will feel better if we get a refund for the lehenga. That too, we got a good discount when I ordered it, knowing how kanjoos my parents are. Like... man... it is their daughter's wedding! Come on... if they can't spend generously on it, then when will they spend... and on what? But that is not my main point.

Okay. Here's my main point — my shaadi got cancelled. Theek hai? That ass cancelled it. Which ass? My fiancé. Rather, my ex-fiancé. I still love that shitty ass — that's the main problem. Even after what he did! All because of bad timing. As if we knew in advance that this corona-sharona rubbish would come like a toofan and destroy the world! We were to marry nicely

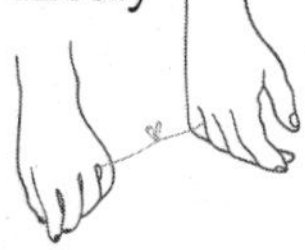

and properly and have a destination wedding.

After a lot of thinking, budgeting and bhashans between the families, we had finalised Colombo because the rates were cheapest there, and at the same time, it was 'abroad-wali shaadi'. We would need passports and visas, vaghera. And most of our relatives didn't mind spending a little more going to Sri Lanka, since they had never been and decided to combine the children's summer vacation with my shaadi. Ditto for my office ke log, and a few close friends. I had spent hours and hours, like reallllly slaved, to get good rates for everything.

My fiancé – oh – his name is Ruchir, didn't bother one bit. He'd left all arrangements to me. 'Yaar... it's your call. You handle it.' I was so touched and flattered! He had full faith in me, my tastes and my judgment.

His parents also agreed and told my Pappaji, 'Dekhiyeji, the shaadi is always from the ladkiwale log in our family. We will come as your mehman. So, we leave all arrangements to you, ji. You just have to hand us our airline tickets – bas! Baat khatam.'

My parents took it in the right spirit. I was the last daughter to marry off, and they wanted to be free of all responsibilities after my shaadi. This was understood by me, and I wasn't being unreasonable at all. Both my sisters had enjoyed a full on, dhoom dhadaka Panju wedding, but I knew when it was my turn, I would have to compromise. Pappaji was still paying off the earlier debts from those two traditional, arranged marriages. Ruchir was also most understanding. He kept saying, 'Jaanu, I want to marry you – I don't care about anything else. Let's not spoil things by discussing budgets, vaghera.'

I told him firmly, 'But we have to discuss a few basics, na? My Pappaji can only spend what he is comfortable with spending at this stage.'

Ruchir smiled 'that' smile of his and said, 'Dude... you are too hot, yaar. Just pull your bra down, na? I want to see your tits.'

Ruchir was like that only. Every time we needed to talk seriously, he would turn sexy and avoid the topic. But I had fallen for him big time, na? I didn't see through his tricks.

That way, Mummyji was much more shaani – she told me straightaway after meeting him, 'Munda changa hai. Job-wob sab theek thaak... but solid nahi lagta.' I was furious!

I asked her, 'Solid ka matlab?' But she shook her head and kept quiet. This was soon after he had proposed, and I had eagerly accepted. I mean... Ruchir was quite a catch in our social circles. Ex-bureaucrat ka ladla puttar. Handsome, flirty, six pack... he was trying out a new business, a small Chinese restaurant in Noida. Really small. Serving that yummy Chinjabi khaana office workers love... It was taking off nicely... and then the lockdown happened, and he got screwed. He had to shut down, like everyone else... he had borrowed money to start the place, so naturally he was very tense about the future.

Our future.

It was not his fault this virus had come out of the blue and ruined all businesses. Suddenly, his income came down to zero... and his mood changed. Besides, we could not meet since I was stuck in Delhi and he was with his parents outside the city limits. Had we met during this awful period, I am sure all the issues that came up because of this Covid nonsense would have worked out between us. There were so many things that had to be finalised about our shaadi, now that Sri Lanka was out. We needed to fix a new date, and cancel all our bookings.

'I leave it to you.' Ruchir had said indifferently, when I brought it up, once we knew we would have to reschedule and rebook events. But after that first conversation, when I was too shocked to even express my disappointment about the postponed shaadi fully, he stopped talking about the wedding altogether.

I also didn't push it, knowing he had a lot on his mind — what with 'Mr. Chinaman' shutting down abruptly. I told him I was likely to get laid off myself — we were in the same boat. And he snapped, 'Dude... drop it, yaar! What shaaadi shaadi shaadi... where's the money to get married? All you chicks can only thing of one thing — marriage! See what the world is going through! We are all bloody broke, yaar. The economy has tanked. People are crying everywhere. There's no fucking money in the market for anything. India is bloody fucked, yaar. Another five years of this — take it from me. All that bullshit about stimulus package and what not. Where is the fucking package, I ask you? Where is the money?'

Maybe Ruchir had a point. I tried to reason with him that everybody was feeling bad. But that didn't mean people had stopped getting married!

I told him sweetly, 'Don't worry about the money, Jaanu... we will scale it all down. Do a simple wedding without any extra ceremonies. Just our two families and a few friends.' He pretended he had not heard me and changed the subject.

I was already making calls to a few wedding planners — the chhota mota ones, and looking for venues close to our home. Since the trousseau had been ordered well in advance, I didn't have to worry on that front. I had organised Ruchir's clothes along with mine — it was just more convenient. And that way we could colour co-ordinate our looks. It's important to plan properly — especially for Insta and all that. We had to look amazzzzzzzing in our videos.

Why not, yaar? Half the fun of getting married was to make others 'j' – hai ki nahi? Be honest! Ruchir was so sporting and sweet, he didn't interfere or make any fuss. He said, 'Dude... you know I look great in anything. Worry about yourself! And hit the gym... okay?' He always teased me about my hips and thighs. Not in a bad way, but I did feel conscious, especially when I had especially dressed up for him and he'd take one look at my outfit and say, 'Shakira... Hips don't lie!'

Anyways... now I was stuck with all these expensive clothes.

And I didn't know what to do with them. Ruchir had stopped taking my calls. He had Unfollowed me on Insta. I was like... devastated! What mistake had I made? What crime had I committed? How could he just block me? Why? Mummyji tried to console me, but she was no good at it.

In fact, she made me feel worse by repeating, 'Beta... I had told you from the beginning... this boy is tedha, not straight and honest. But did you listen? Now look!'

Pappaji was quiet and didn't want to get drawn into anything emotional. He only asked, 'How will we get refunds?'

I felt really bad. Here I was feeling depressed, unable to sleep at night, swallowing all sorts of pills... and missing my Ruchir! My wedding had been cancelled without any explanation, and all my parents cared about were refunds. Mummyji found me crying in the room a few nights ago. She came and sat next to me.

'Beta... it is better this has happened now,' she said, trying to console me. My lehenga was hung up on the curtain rod, wrapped in a plastic cover. Next to it, was Ruchir's matching sherwani. Both had summer flowers on it, like those Abu-Jani outfits worn by the Bachchans. Delhi karigars were good at copying designer wear, though the Amritsar ones who specialised in duplicate designer outfits were the best — remember Anushka's pink wedding lehenga? Mine was even better!

I stared at it and my tears would not stop. If I could have, I would have got into Pappaji's car and driven straight to Noida, with the lehenga and sherwani on the backseat, and my wedding jewellery in velvet boxes. I was willing to defy all orders, break the lockdown, risk arrest... but just go! I wanted to meet Ruchir face to face. I wanted to confront him — show him all my beautiful shopping.

I was sure he would change his mind, smile his Ruchir smile if he saw me (I had lost weight, but not because of gymming, I was just too upset to eat!), and he'd say, 'Jaanu... let's do it! Come on jaanu... pick up your top, lower your straps... show me those juicy tits.'

Ha! It was my turn now! I would laugh in his face and say, 'Go fuck yourself! My tits are too precious to waste them on a kachrapatti, ghatiya man like you! Only my husband can enjoy them in the future — got it? Wait for my wedding card. And here's your bloody achkan... I got it for next to nothing. You think you are the only cheap person in the world? You thought you had fooled me with that fake diamondwalli engagement ring? My mummyji is too shaani also. She had it tested... We were planning to give you a fake one at the wedding, too!'

A PRESSURE COOKER ROMANCE

My neighbour's pressure cooker always annoyed me. God knows what that family ate and how many times, but I would hear that whistle at least twenty times a day — when I was home, that is. My life was different, being a field worker and all that. I don't call myself an activist as such, because people get put off and become suspicious.

I just say, 'I am a research scholar'. It sounds better. I like to mind my own business and don't let anybody poke their noses into mine. When I travel, I just lock my place and go. It is a small flat. Some would say it is very small. But my needs are minimal. I don't cook at all. So maybe that is why that pressure cooker whistle bugs me. After the lockdown, I am stuck in this cramped space. And since I have never kept food stuff at home, I have been inconvenienced a lot. How much bread and butter can I eat and how often? I was used to drinking cutting chai when I was on the road. Sugary chai, which gave me the energy to keep walking.

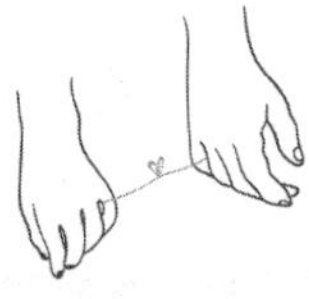

This is terrible! And each time I hear that whistle, it forces me to think of food. I don't like feeling hungry and craving something which is out of my reach. That is how I have disciplined myself over the years. I need water — clean water. And tea. That's enough for me. My colleagues used to find it odd that my kitchen stocked nothing — not even salt and sugar. What would I do with either when I had no use for all that? I didn't believe in allowing my body to become dependent on such superficial requirements. I was happy to eat street food if necessary — vada pav was always available. And I kept biscuits in my handbag, since I had low blood pressure and had fainted during field work once or twice.

My 'Sir' (I never call him by name) is a good person and keeps telling me, 'Eat eat eat ...' I smile and lie, 'I have eaten at home and come to work.' Each time I think of food, I hear that pressure cooker whistle! These days I have started to hear it in my sleep. In fact, I have become obsessed by that sound — and miss it when there is a long gap between the whistles. That may be because it is the only sound I hear in the midst of this deathly silence. The road outside is normally so noisy, with several vendors going about here and there, up and down this gully, shouting and letting people know they have arrived. Someone who sharpens knives, another who collects old clothes in exchange for stainless steel glasses.

I am accustomed to their cries. But with this lockdown, there is only silence. Even the stray dogs in the area have stopped barking. Everybody is so scared. Too scared if you ask me. I cannot see a soul on the little lane that leads to the bigger gully.

I wonder where those people have disappeared? They don't come to their windows, forget balconies. What do they think — that this coronavirus is an eagle that will swoop from the sky and gouge out their eyes? Ignorant people, I tell you.

Oh God! There goes the whistle. I counted... this is the seventh one since morning. Should I complain that the noise disturbs my sleep? How will it sound? That lady may ask, 'Who sleeps till 11.30 in the morning?' I do! Any problem? My choice when to get up — there is nothing to get up for!

Except Sir's phone. Yes, that is important. But I don't know when he is going to phone, or even if he will call. It is not a fixed thing. Sir calls to check on me, he says. I suppose he must be worried — what if I get corona and die? Nobody will let him know. And then he'll have to look for a new research assistant. These days, that's not easy. Nobody wants to do field work and go inside slums. I am used to it, so I don't mind. Especially on days when Sir also comes and we go from house to house asking questions.

Sometimes, the sex-workers in these slums ask Sir if I am his wife. He smiles and keeps quiet. I am not sure if Sir has a wife. I think he does not, or he would have mentioned it indirectly, especially now that he phones me, and it is not always about work. Sir said the lockdown is a good opportunity to understand life more deeply. He always says such encouraging things. Last week Sir also heard the pressure cooker whistle when he phoned to ask about the data I had collected.

He asked, 'I thought you said you don't cook? But I just heard a pressure cooker whistle.' I felt most embarrassed. And also happy — Sir had remembered my stray remark! I got a little nervous and started stammering, 'No, Sir… I mean, yes, Sir… that is… it is not my whistle. My neighbour is whistling, not me, Sir.' He was silent and then he started to laugh. It was the first time I had heard Sir laugh. So even I laughed. We both laughed for a good minute or so. The pressure cooker whistle had done the trick!

Sir told me he would take me to his favourite snack bar once the lockdown was lifted. 'After we go together on the next field trip to Pune.' Had I heard right? Sir and me will be travelling to Pune? I closed my eyes and tried not to think too much. Just then the neighbour's pressure cooker whistled again. I took it as a good omen.

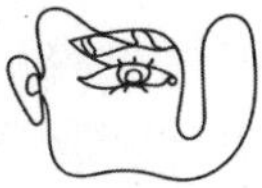

FROM POMEGRANATES TO LOVE LETTERS

I had always wanted to write a love letter to my dream man. Unfortunately, neither my dream nor my man had materialised. I was 26 years old… and still to fall in love. Like properly fall in love — full on! No holding back. That kind of love. I had flirted with a few guys in college, and later, at work. But love as I imagined it to be, had still to happen. I think it was the pomegranate juice that helped me fall in love achchi tarah! Don't laugh! I always had pomegranate juice at the juice centre opposite my office, from the same juicewala, who would start looking for good pomegranates as soon as he spotted me making my way towards his stall while walking to Churchgate station, generally around 7.30 p.m.

I used to do a time-pass job in a stockbroker's firm on Dalal Street. My job was ok — just ok. I was a commerce graduate, and my parents were not that well-off that I could afford to waste time without earning as soon as I finished college. Of course, my lamba plan was to go for a proper MBA degree to a good university in England or America. I had applied nicely

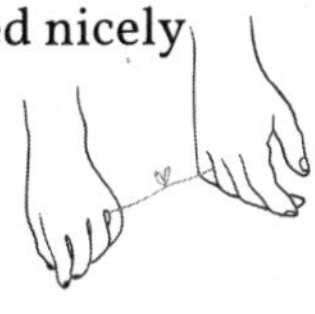

with the help of a colleague, and saved up also. Didn't want to ask my parents for money — Mummy and Papa were so proud of me already! I was the first person to graduate from our small community, and even though my family has always lived in Mumbai, most of our relatives were still in our ancestral village in Gujarat. Oh, I forgot to give my name — myself, Anmol. My Ba chose the name, because I was the first son and she said I was too precious — no value could be put on me! I lost my Ba recently, and I still cry when I remember her.

The juicewala was a nice man, and always asked me for market tips — which stocks to buy, which to sell, like that type tips. I used to wonder why a juicewala would want to invest in the market — but still, I would tell him what I had overheard during trading hours that day. Sometimes, my tips were too good! And he would make good money — next day, he wouldn't charge for the pomegranate juice. But if he lost money because of me, he would make me buy him a vada pav from the man who had a stall down the road from him. It was a good friendship, I should say. We had trust and understanding.

There were hundreds of boys and girls just like me on Dalal Street. We worked hard and came from decent homes. Some of us took the same train and had friendly relationships. We helped each other also, and exchanged market gossip. Even though we were competitors. That way, brokers are very informal — we share what we hear, and everybody benefits.

I met Vikas like that only... at the juicewala's. He also loved pomegranate juice and only drank that. Like me.

We started our friendship discussing pomegranate juice. Whether it is good for health, whether to add ice cubes to it in summer, whether to mix it with any other juice, whether some pomegranates were better than others, whether to go for foreign pomegranates or stick to Indian only — so much to think and discuss about the subject! So many varieties to choose from! I confessed to Vikas that if I drank pomegranate juice every single day for four days, on the fifth day, I got constipation.

He said, 'Oh my God! I thought I was the only one! I also have same to same problem.' We gave high fives... and that was the day we hugged for the first time! And laughed like anything. So much we laughed and laughed that my stomach started to pain. I looked at my watch — arrey! I'd missed my fast train to Jogeshwari. Mummy would be waiting. Papa also. Food would get cold. Mummy would have to heat all the shaakh-bhaaji again. Make fresh rotlis. I felt very bad. But... very good also. I really liked that first hug so much, so much, I can't tell you. Vikas had such a nice soft body... really! Like a pillow! The pillow on my bed at home was very hard and lumpy. I never used to get good sleep because of it, but I didn't complain. Why to complain and make people feel bad?

Since I had missed the train any way, I looked at Vishal and he looked at me. The juicewala looked at us. We were smiling into each other's eyes, Vishal and me. The juicewala was staring at us as if he knew something. That evening, the juicewala did not ask me for any share bazaar tips. I did not give, also. Even though I had a few. My mind and heart were lost. My thinking, also — fully gone. My feet... I still had my feet? I was not sure! I felt like a gas balloon on Chowpatty Beach, simply floating and floating. I said to Vishal, just like that, 'Let's go to Marine Drive and look at Malabar Hill.'

He laughed and said, 'I see Malabar Hill everyday...'

I asked, 'How? Why?'

He answered, 'Because I live there...' I felt stupid also and impressed also. If he lived there — he was rich or what? Didn't look so rich. Meaning, he looked like me only — normal shirt-pant type. His phone was also a dabba android. Not a fancy rich boy's phone. Meaning, iPhone. Shoes were usual, Colaba-Bandra type shoes. Not fancy or anything. I looked at him properly — up down, up down. No! Nothing different. Not rich looking, as such.

Vishal saw me staring at him and put his hand on my shoulder, 'Darr gaya kya?' he asked with a smile. I felt funny standing on the road, with the juicewala staring and staring.

So I also smiled, and said, 'Why darr gaya? For what? You are not a mad dog who can bite, na? Chalo... let's go to Marine Drive. You keep your eyes shut if you want and not look at Malabar Hill because you are a big shot and live there. I will look at everything — from Nariman Point, to Chowpatty to Raj Bhavan... okay?'

Acchha, before you get some galat impression... all this

happened before the coronavirus. Some of us had started calling it 'Vireless'... it sounded cute. Once the Modiwala lockdown happened, I had to sit at home haath jod ke and cry... aur kya? Dhanda bandh. Sab kuch bandh. Aur Vikas? Bataa raha hoon.

Back to my love story...

After our eyes met over those red-red pomegranates, I am telling frankly, my heart started going dhak-dhak, dhak-dhak... like that Madhuri Dixit song. Vikas and I strolled off from the juicewala holding hands, khullam khulla. So, I knew he didn't mind me! We smiled and giggled, not looking left or right at anybody. Not caring! Bindaas! The distance to Marine Drive was hardly 15 minutes away from Dalal Street. During that short walk, we told each other so much! Looking back I think I shared much more than he shared. I wanted to keep talking and smiling, doing more bakbak. Vikas told me he didn't like working with his Papa. I asked 'Why?'

He replied, 'Too much interference... no private time for...' I nodded my head to agree even though I did not agree. What private time did a son need from his own Papa — for what? While walking slowly slowly to Marine Drive, we stopped in front of Gaylord's... I had never entered that restaurant. See... where I come from, we eat simple nashta, made by Mummy or Ba. And we enjoy sandwichwala ka sandwich — vegetable and green chutney and boiled potatoes. On Dalal Street, there were many dosawalas selling Chinese dosas and Italian dosas, also pizza with chowmein on top. But I didn't waste money on such things. I gave my earnings to my Papa. Vishal told me he didn't do that. And I was a little surprised.

I said to him confidently, 'Shall we have coffee at Gaylord's?' I said it like I came there every week. He said, 'Why not?' I had not checked how much money I had in my pocket, so I quickly said, 'Today, let's go to Marine Drive only... tomorrow, Gaylord's... okay?'

He nodded and waved 'Hi-bye' to some man in a checked shirt who was passing. Even though I shouldn't have asked, I blurted out, 'Who's he?' — trying to keep the jealousy out of my voice. Vishal laughed, 'Just... someone...' I left his hand and felt bad. Vishal reached out and again held my hand. Tighter this time. As if he did not want to let me go. I felt too good! I quickly forgot the man in the checked shirt and squeezed Vikak's hand.

After some time, walking-walking slowly in silence, Vikas asked in a friendly voice, 'You must be getting lots of inside market info, right? Which new issues coming and all that? My papa also gets... he audits many big-big companies...'

I smiled. Even the fruitwala used to ask me for share bazaar tips... now Vishal, also. It made me feel important. So I said, 'Haan haan... arrey... everyday someone is giving hot tips — everyday!' Vishal reached out and pinched my cheek, 'I find you only hot, meri jaan!'

So like this only, we became close, exchanged numbers,

all that in a very decent way. And, of course, we met at the juicewala for pomegranate juice. It became our regular meeting place.

Sometimes, I managed to taste Vishal's tongue quickly after the juice. When nobody was looking. Once or twice the juicewala caught us and frowned. I didn't care! I only cared for Vishal. Yes, he had asked for a small loan to settle some transaction. I gave it to him. He was not just any casual friend — we called each other Jaan. And listened to 'Chaudvi ka Chaand', sitting on Marine Drive, looking towards Vishal's Malabar Hill home.

I once asked him, 'Show me your building... which one is it?' He had pointed to a tall tower in the distance, just behind the Raj Bhavan, and said, 'That building.' I stared and stared. There were 30, 40, 50 buildings... all looked the same. But I said, 'Ohhhhh... so wonderful... so nice... so tall. Fifty-sixty floors... easy... right? Wah wah wah... my building is only four-five floors, Jaan!' We clicked a few selfies and all that. Everyone clicks selfies on the Marine Drive parapet. I was too excited, too excited!

First time I was clicking romantic selfies, while feeling romantic. That way, I had many selfies with casual friends. But those were not with real feelings — just naam ke waastey, to impress on Insta and FB. I used to get many 'likes', and also feel hurt when people posted bad things, calling me 'gandu' and such words. I should have asked Vikas before posting... but two things happened at the same time — Modiji announced the

Janta Curfew on a Sunday... and I posted our selfies the same night! Had I known it would upset Vikas so much, so much — would I have done it?

He called and fired me like anything! I started crying. Mummy came running, Daddy came running... they thought I was upset that the market would crash and we would all be ruined! Put on the street. Then they thought I was crying thinking coronavirus will kill all of us. How to tell them the truth about my heart — I could see it lying in my thaali! It was looking so bad, my heart, black in parts and divided up like this and like that. But still beating and beating. I wanted it to stop beating! I was fully dead. I did not need a heart any more. It was such a useless heart. Vikas cut the call while I was still crying.

Mummy made me drink chhaas to cool my system. She said it is important to keep cool — Modiji was also saying the same. I was too much disturbed — what crime had I committed? By posting our together-wala selfies, I wanted to share our beautiful love story with the world. Share our happiness. Why Vikas got so much gussa with me? Why? There were so many questions I wanted to ask Vikas... I tried to phone him, knowing he would not pick up. He cut my calls. I was prepared to wait. Then Vikas did something I did not expect — he blocked me.

That was the night I began writing love letters to Vikas. My lockdown love letters. I write one letter a day. Sometimes in the morning, sometimes late at night. My feelings are getting stronger and stronger. I want Vikas to know me inside out. So that when I ask him to marry me, there will be no secrets from my side. Vikas doesn't know it now, but he will find out. I will not give up so easily. So what if he doesn't want to talk to me? So what if we cannot meet because of the lockdown? One day... someday, Modiji will see sense and lift the lockdown.

And after that, once again Vikas and I will drink pomegranate juice at the juicewala and kiss on the Marine Drive parapet.

NO CHICKEN PLEASE

Deva! Deva! Madamji is asking for chicken again! I don't know what to tell her. Madamji knows this is a strictly vegetarian home. We are poor people. Even if she pays for the chicken it cannot be brought inside our house. Where will she eat that chicken? Sitting on the footpath outside? We are very strict with our khaana peena. I don't even eat lasoon! Forget chicken-wicken. Yes, Baba. I am a devout follower of my Devi. I took a vow not to touch meat, eggs, chicken when I became her devotee after my children started falling ill one by one. Deviji also asked me to give up one more daily use food item I enjoyed eating. And I chose lasoon. I could have chosen sugar or rice — that would have at least kept my weight down. But I didn't think of it at that time and picked garlic, which I was very partial to. So, in that sense, I didn't deceive my Deviji at all. Giving up lasoon was my own wish. My own sacrifice. It was a mannat I took when my son was very sick. Now the boy is doing well in school, keeps good health and I can relax a little.

But for the constant bak bak bak of my Madamji. She is a

non-stop talker. From the time she opens her eyes till she falls asleep — she even talks to herself when nobody is around. It's her old habit. But this frequent demand for chicken is annoying me. Arrey baba… who thinks of eating chicken morning, noon and night? That too, during a lockdown, when people are dying right and left of corona?

I explained to her nicely, 'Madamji, please be understanding and patient. Once you go back to your own home and your cook starts coming on duty again, you can eat your Punjabi chicken every day, twice a day. But now that you are stuck in my small room… please try to understand my problem. I cannot bring chicken inside this room. Or my boy will fall sick again. He may get corona. And if he gets infected, so will you. And if you get infected at your advanced age, well… frankly, you will not survive. Nobody will give you a bed in any hospital. Not even the big big very expensive ones which charge more than a lakh for one night inside the ICU. Ventilator and other kharcha on medicines and masks and all that, is extra. All the wards are over full, Madamji. Dead bodies are lying here and there… in the corridors, on the beds. Cremations have to be postponed — where to burn so many bodies? Do you really want to "off" just like that? No, na?'

How much to samjhao her? First of all, Madamji is 87 years old… and she has soooooo many health problems. Too much khit pit, that too, non-stop. Yeh lao. Yeh do. Yeh karo. No other Maushi had lasted with her. Everyone said she was too bossy and raised her voice constantly. Nobody wanted to work for this katkati woman. Also, she used dirty English gaalis thinking we won't understand! We all know the meaning of 'Bitch' and 'Swine' and 'Bastard'. I was warned about her by the building watchman.

He had said, 'That fourth floor wali buddhi is a pagal aurat. Bhoot type. Talks to herself and fights with everyone. Servants don't last in her flat for more than a week – good luck!'

When she opened the door, I did not expect to see such a tiny, shrunken woman. I suppose her loud voice on the phone when she interviewed me, gave the impression she was a huge lady. Anyway, I had come through an agency which supplied Maushis to people like her, and other patients who did not want to spend on day and night nurses, but could not manage on their own, either. I have been working as a Maushi for 35 years. Which means I am as good as any of those qualified nurses from Kerala. But I don't have a degree and I cannot wear that smart nurses-wala starched white uniform.

I wear sarees. Good sarees, mind you. I like to appear neat and efficient when I am on duty. That way, I get more respect. I am just a Maushi – I assist qualified nurses, some of whom are younger than my youngest daughter, who is 23 and lives in Mumbai with her husband. With my long experience as a Maushi I know much more than these bachcha nurses. I can do their job better than them. But I keep mum. Especially when the doctors come on visits. I can answer all their questions. But I don't interfere. The nurses don't like it if I show off my knowledge.

I am aware of my good qualities. If this Madamji had not kept me, I would have easily got another job — experienced Maushis are always in demand. Surprisingly, Madamji liked my personality and approach. She told me she would keep me on a trial basis for a week, and then decide. That was nine years ago! I understood Madamji's needs very quickly. She required a Maushi to stay eight hours with her, as she couldn't go to the bathroom on her own, and, also, she needed help while bathing.

At night, she kept a proper Kerala nurse to give her a bed pan, and nebuliser because of her breathing difficulties, check her blood pressure, monitor her sugar levels, give her an injection if needed, make sure she took her anti-anxiety pills, see that her blanket was properly fixed and all that. This system had worked out well for both of us. Madamji was a very wealthy lady. Everybody in the locality knew her. They used to make fun of her for being stingy even though she had so much money. But she was okay with me. And in any case her London-wali daughter paid for everything.

I soon became a part of her household. We had a fixed routine after I reported for work at 8 a.m. and relieved the night nurse. I won't bore you with all those details, but this is to say I knew Madamji inside out. All her habits were known to me — from the way she liked her fruit to be cut and served, to the toilet paper brand she preferred. How can there be any secrets when two people live with each other so closely, with one person completely dependent on the other for everything?

I treated Madamji like my baby — I fed her, bathed her, cleaned her, changed her clothes, combed her hair, cut her toe nails, entertained her by singing her favourite songs, watched the TV news and a few Hindi serials with her, helped her pay her bills , accompanied her to the bank and grocery store. Sometimes we went to her hair salon, where she had a regular manicure-pedicure appointment. Since she didn't like walking with a stick, she would place her left hand on my right shoulder as we crossed the road, or went for a small stroll in the nearby garden. If we went for a drive, she would eat ice cream on the way home. She was chalega that way — she would get ice cream for me and the driver as well — but smaller cups for us, and a large one for herself.

All was going smoothly, till the lockdown was announced on 24th March. Madamji's night nurse called to say she wouldn't be able to come any longer, till this lockdown and curfew was lifted. Madamji was stunned! She went completely blank and disconnected the phone. She then looked at me sternly and said, 'That's it then. If the night nurse cannot come, you cannot go. How will I manage on my own? You have to stay!'

I thought quickly — and told her firmly, 'Madamji... you know very well I cannot stay the night anywhere. My husband and I have an understanding. My boy is only ten, he needs me. I have to cook for both of them. My salary keeps my kitchen fires burning. And if I stay here tonight, I will be stuck for God knows how many days! It is impossible.'

She hobbled to where I was standing. I thought she was going to slap me. But no! She took me completely off guard! Madamji changed her domineering personality just like that. Next minute, she was pleading... her voice had become that of a little child. She lowered her eyes, stood before me, bowed her head, joined her hands and said, 'I BEG of you. I will pay anything you ask for. I will give you enough money.... jewellery... educate your boy, even get your useless husband a job in my friend's house. But you cannot walk away and leave me alone.'

Then she started crying... howling. My Madam! I couldn't believe what I was seeing. Before I could react, she fell at my feet, 'If you leave tonight, you won't be able to return at all till the lockdown is lifted. Nobody else will be able to enter my home either. The rules are very strict. Who will look after me? Help me. I will starve and die a dog's death.'

I didn't know what to do or say. I was so embarrassed by my Madam touching my feet. I told her to call her daughter in London and ask her what to do. Madamji tried several times but the daughter did not take the call. I had a few minutes to think coolly and take a decision. I took it on my own without consulting my husband or son. While she was dialing London again, I told her in a clear firm voice, 'Madamji, there is only one solution.'

She looked up, the tears were still rolling down her cheeks. I said, 'I cannot stay here with you.' She started to howl and clutch my saree. Then I added, 'But you can come and stay with me.' Madamji was too shocked at first. Her mouth was open and she was just staring and staring.

I thought she would shout at me for suggesting something so ridiculous! How could such a big, well-known Madamji residing in a luxury flat come and live in a Maushi's small little house located inside a very crowded locality? She paused. She must have been making some calculations.

Then, she wiped her tears quickly, looked me straight in the eye and said slowly, 'You are absolutely right. There is no other choice, is there? Either I go with you, or I stay here and die. I am not ready to die. Come on… don't waste so much time gazing stupidly at me. What are you waiting for? Get on with it and start packing. I will tell you which nighties to put into my suitcase. Take the old bag. Why take the other foreign one to your… your… '

I knew she wanted to say 'Your small and dirty, little home in the slums'. But she is smart that way — my Madamji! She kept quiet and smiled. 'I will be nice to your husband, don't worry. Your boy, too. What's his name? And do let him know your salary is doubled from this month. And haan, please take only my rubber chappals. Leave the leather sandals here. I won't be needing them for some time. Listen — I hope you have a western style toilet, that too, inside your house? Not a filthy common loo?'

I didn't reply. Let her find out for herself what we have and what we don't.

Imagine! She has been stuck inside a poor person's home — mine — for more than two months! Eating what we eat, sleeping on a cot my husband gave up for her, using our Indian style toilet, drinking our type of tea. Who would believe such a story! Madamji... living with a Maushi in her kholi. Because the option was a lonely death as a rich lady in a huge flat with nobody to look after her. No chicken in her own house. No chicken in my house. Her only wish nowadays! I am feeling sorry for Madamji. On her last day here once the lockdown ends, I will get my neighbour to prepare a komdi dish for her. My husband has agreed to pay for it. I will pack it up in a plastic dabba — how can I give it in my husband's steel tiffin box? It will get polluted by chicken and I will have to throw it away. Plastic is best. Then, I will request my husband's taxiwala friend to come here to fetch madamji. Once she reaches home, she can sit at her round, glass dining table and eat chicken aaram se, with a knife and fork and all that. What a strange situation, you must be thinking. But the times are also strange, na?

BEACH HOUSE BIRTHDAY

'Oye... where are you guys? Come and watch the cyclone... it's pretty awesome.' Idiots! Must be bloody lolling around watching some dumbass shows. Jesus! Just my luck I had to get stuck with this bunch of losers. This is my fucking set-up... it was meant to be a chilled out weekend bringing in my wife's thirtieth — not this shitty lockdown crap of getting locked in with her stupid galpal chamchis.

Gawd! One stupider than the other. Them — and me! Thank God we have our staff staying with us... or else, I swear I would have started swimming back to Mumbai as soon as we got the news about the lockdown happening. Even when we heard it, I didn't take it seriously. I said to my staff, 'Dekha jayega, guys...' and I got myself a drink. See... had all of us been given proper time to get organised, we would have managed somehow. But come on... what the fuck could we do from Awas at 8 p.m. on a fucking Sunday, that too? I love my set-up here and all that. But this place is a village, okay? And the jetty in Mandwa is not in my backyard. We still have to drive there to catch a boat

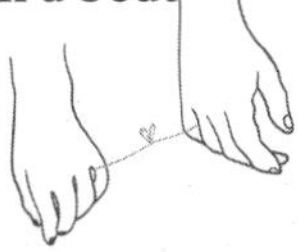

back to Mumbai. Upar se, Mandwa is not Monaco, that we can just jump into a speedboat from our private jetty and bugger off. Idhar toh there is bhaari security and stuff. Besides, the boats weren't plying, the sea was closed. Had Shah Rukh been in my place, even he would not have been able to do a thing! And imagine King Khan and I are almost like neighbours here in Alibaug! Not aamney samne... my beach house is in Awas and his is close by in another village, but still, yaar, we are neighbours here.

Driving back was also out. I checked. Called my cop friends — yeah, yeah, the same ones I go dance for like a trained monkey at the annual police event. Shit man! I mean, we could have got our shit together and left for Mumbai, like a few people did. But who was sane that night? I bloody couldn't get my head straight. Had done stuff... plus, all those shots... nothing was making sense. Those women were on some other trip... in some other zone. Honestly speaking, we really thought we could do the usual setting the next morning... bribe a few cops. Bas.

But this fucking party was not meant to end that way... or that quickly. By the time we woke up, it was two in the afternoon. My manager had called a hundred times. I still didn't think we were going to be stuck here. I phoned Mr. Fixer — everybody's favourite cop. Pandayji said, 'No chance!'

He said, 'Sorry boss... orders. You will need special permission to cross districts and enter the city. Not safe. Stay there, only. Have fun! Relax... eat... mauj karo. All are in the same boat, Arnavji!'

Have fun my ass! Birthday-shirthday was okay. I could explain all this party shit to Ema. She is also not that thick to throw attitude for something like this. I mean, come on... Shams and I have been married for six years — dated for four. Ten years, yaar! We have been together for a fucking decade. Shams was there when I was a fucking nobody — just another chikna chap from Bhopal desperate to get into Bollywood.

Whatever may have gone wrong later, she was fucking there, solidly behind me, even when her parents wanted her to break off and marry that paisawala Marwari fucker from Kolkata. I may be a low class harami, but I can't forget all that and ignore her big birthday. Shams hadn't asked for anything impossible — she just wanted to celebrate it at this home in Alibaug with her friends — you know, style mein, champagne-wampagne ke saath. Why not, yaar? Big deal. Shams was not like that those other bitches from the star wives brigade. I was shocked at some of the crazy demands these women made. Woh meri heroine from Door Ho Jao, that sexy Sanam, yaar, had told me she had given an ultimatum to Rehan — 'I want a Rolls and a 7-carat pink ...' And that bloody fool husband had given her the ring, but told her to settle for a Porsche, not a Rolls. She had said, 'How cheap!' Yeah... Our industry is like this only. You have to keep the wives khushhhhh.

When I brought up Shams' birthday plan, my woman, Ema, sweetly said, 'Okay baby... go for one night... I will manage. A birthday is a birthday. You both have to do it for Insta and all that... I am cool with it.' She is smart, that girl. Most of these safed chamdi chicas hanging around on the sets are very smart. Russians are all over the place. Achha Ukrainians... Lithuanians... Estonians... Latvians... by now, I know all the different countries they come from. Mine is from Slovenia. Ema keeps showing off and telling everybody her family is related to Melania Trump. As if!

Not that I care. And in our business, nobody wants to know where these girls come from. So long as they exist! And they give. I met Ema at a party — my producer had wanted to celebrate the success of 'Jaanu', our big hit. Or so he said. God knows — maybe he had laid a new chick or fathered a son somewhere. We were in the middle of our new shoot — the sequel to 'Jaanu'. I was going to skip his rubbish party — no lines, cheap booze, and wall-to-wall hookers. But I had to go to show my face. And there she was — Ema! Three inches taller than me... taut butt, blond... like those James Bond type girls.

Yaaar... come on... I am a man, okay? Not just any man. I am a hero in Bollywood — nine fucking hits. No jokes. I am big! Like... people know who the fuck I am wherever I go. Not just in India... Pakistan, Sri Lanka, Malaysia, Singapore, London, Toronto. And this fucking girl stared blankly at me — like I was a nobody. Or some chhota mota side-hero. Khair... I got her a G and T, just like that, to lagao an impression. I didn't act cheap. I can be very classy, okay? She smiled and all that, and let me touch her hair without fussing... that's my test with chicks I dig — will they freak out if I touch their hair at our first meeting or not? If they freak — out they go. When she didn't slap my hand away, I knew I was majorly into her.

I could tell she was also interested, but she came across as a seasoned player, even though she was pretty young... and looked it. Not fixed up or anything. No work done on her nose or chin or jawline. I assumed she was one more back-up dancer — there are hundreds of them on the sets during our big productions. But she told me she had a double degree in finance. No shit! And that she had landed a good job with a big production house after working in London with a media setup.

Hmmmm. Finance. Sexy. And a great butt. Okayyyyy. Ema knew her numbers and played poker professionally. I told Shams about her the same night! And Shams had given me that knowing wifewala look. Shams had more or less stopped coming to these filmi parties with me, so she paid no attention when I went on and on about this Ema and how cool she was... how totally brainy. I am sure I mentioned her butt... maybe not. Anyway, Ema and I started a relationship soon after that party. I got busy with a new movie and it was her production house that stepped in to produce it when the original promoters went bust.

The first shooting schedule was finalised in Monte Negro — a 20 day shoot, I was told. Ema was to accompany the unit and oversee budgets. This is when things got serious. We drove to Arto, her village in Slovenia, over a weekend, and I met her parents, neighbours, aunts, uncles, priest, funeral director, baker, cobbler, hairdresser everyone. We made no secret of our closeness. Not even on social media. Ema posted a picture of us walking through her village, on the banks of the Sava river, holding hands and with her niece in tow. She captioned it, 'Mr.

India with Ms. Slovenia.' I responded with a heart emoji.

Must say I was surprised when Shams flipped out. Rather those chamchi girlfriends instigated her and she created a big hungama like a fool. Had she ignored it nothing would have happened. Come on, yaar. We are actors... this is a part of our lives. Star wives get it — well, most of them do. They understand, yaar. Shams had always got it in the past. Yaaaar... we were married! Shams had my name... full security. I came home to her bed only every night. What more did she want? I denied her nothing! Great Juhu penthouse, club memberships, best gym instructor — personal gym.

And now our amazzzzzing beach bungalow in Alibaug, designed by her bestie. It had been featured in top interiors' magazines and all that. Everybody in the industry was jaloing over it! Burnnnnnning! I tell you.

Those besties of hers were like leeches — they were constantly there! Some had become permanent house guests! We always had two or three floating around our home, which used to bug me. Whenever I came back from a shoot, I would find her girls hanging around, sipping cocktails, having a mani-pedi, basically chilling and living it up at my expense. After a point, I stopped minding or caring or noticing. Where was the time to mind? I worked like a maniac and worked out like a beast. I travelled and travelled and travelled... from one shoot to the next. Shams hasn't wanted to come with me these last few years. She preferred to travel with her bunch of girls — I called them her harem. New York, Los Angeles, London, Paris,

Mykonos. So what yaar? Let them have fun, I used to say. She was a good wife — she stayed out of my life.

Till we found ourselves trapped together on the 24th night without realising that the lockdown would go on and on and on and on. I grew my hair. I grew a beard. I posted pictures working out on the beach. While Salman went riding on his farm and sang songs. Bhai is Bhai. But frankly speaking, I started to panic after two weeks. Then two more weeks. No shooting. No new deals. No calls. I blasted my manager — asked him what the fuck was going on. The people I spoke to said forget it. We are all fucked. The industry is fucked. Where will we show our films? Which theatre? To whom? Who will come to watch? After the fourth week, I lost it. Nobody was reacting to my beard or long hair. And I refused to bake cakes and all that shit. We were all screwed. Ghanta!

And these women! They had bloody run out of clothes and were running around half-nanga all over the place. As if they are in Ibiza... idiots! And they are posing here and there in those ganda bikinis, which have started to stink! Worst of all — they are like wild cats now — fighting and scratching and using foul words non-stop! Shams is also behaving as badly as them. As if it's anybody's bloody fault that one can't get Greek yogurt and quinoa in this village! They are lucky they get garam khaana! My staff is fed up of their non-stop demands for snacks. Such budtameez women, I tell you. The pool is dirty... my beautiful beach home now looks like a fucking Goan shack! Once this thing ends, I am going to tell Shams — it's me or them!

Then came the fucking cyclone! All the satellite pictures showed the landfall happening in Alibaug. I said, 'You fucker! Couldn't you find anywhere else to land but on our heads?' I was worried about Ema – poor baby, all alone in Mumbai, without anybody to help her in case something went wrong and the cyclone lost its fucking way and landed up in Juhu. I watched the cloud formation and told the harem to behave, not go on the beach, and stay out of the pool.

I was desperate to reach Ema, but the signal has always been bad in Alibaug, particularly in our village, because of all those bloody trees. Normally, I would talk to her from the other side of the pool area, out of earshot of the chamchis and Shams. During these days of forced living like this, we had figured out workable equations and found our own zones. My emotional comfort came from the calls Ema and I managed somehow. She was working from home and managing everything efficiently. I was doing jack – nothing! And feeling maha frustrated. I felt it was my duty to check on her – after all, she had become my responsibility, now that we were in an exclusive relationship and I had got her this cute apartment at Bandra. Poor thing was a foreigner... she needed help to deal with local stuff. Her dietary requirements were also tough. I would ask her to call my manager if she ran out of her vegan stuff. My P.R. girl kept calling to say, 'Let's do a proper shoot... you and Ema. We can call the paps to stand outside that organic place you guys grab yogurt from.' But I said have some shame. Show respect to my wife. I know how to behave decently, okay?

Till the lockdown Ema and I had managed well... I had spent weekends with her, and as many days as I could during the week, too. I would land up straight from my shoot and surprise her with chocolates and wine. It was a full-on romance, baba. Sometimes her parents would call when I was there and ask her when we were getting married.

I told her straight, 'No chance, babe! In Bollywood, we don't believe in divorce. Nobody divorces anybody. No matter what. We just carry on.' A few fights had happened because of this issue. But Ema was not the nagging type, thank God. And she had not given me any ultimatums, as such. Shams and her harem tried to bitch her out to me several times during this Alibaug stay, reading other people's Insta posts and putting two and two together to make 25. But I was in no mood to listen to their cheap gossip.

Anyway I watched the cyclone clouds and started missing Ema pagal ke jaisey. Before we were hit by the fucking storm, I rushed to my favourite spot near the far corner of the pool, which was filled with fallen leaves and coconuts from the trees surrounding it — the winds were really strong now, and the electricity had suddenly gone.

The harem was screeching with excitement and saying, 'Oh My God... babes... I think we are all going to die.' Miraculously, I managed to get through to Ema... I wanted to tell her I loved her, just in case the harem was right and we would all die in the cyclone. Her number rang five times — I counted. And when it was picked up, I heard Ema's voice telling someone, 'Don't! It's that asshole! He's in Alibaug… and that's where the cyclone is headed.' Ema was wrong. For once, her calculations were totally off. The cyclone had spared me, spared my beach house, spared Alibaug. But it would not spare her. I would fucking show her what my personal cyclone was capable of, once the lockdown was lifted.

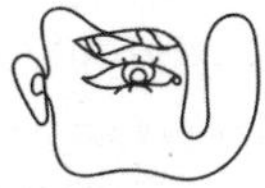

THE MAN WHO WANTED MORE

I have always seen myself as a very successful fellow. Right from my school days. Everyone admired me — my parents, my neighbours, my teachers. So, you see, I didn't really have a complex, as such. I mean, what they call an 'inferiority complex'. All was going well — my job, my status, everything! Till I met my future wife.

Mind you, she was a good woman. I mean, she is still a good woman. But somewhere she lacked something, and I was not sure what that was. Yes, it was an arranged marriage — all of us in the family had arranged marriages. It is better that way, we believe. Why take risks with unknown elements — you get what I mean? We are openly orthodox and conservative — why hide it? Gotra and all that matters to us. We stay in a Brahmin-only colony. Of course, we don't say that to outsiders. But within our community, it is understood that we don't allow non-Brahmins to buy a flat. Non-Brahmins, mind you. Muslims don't stand a chance! Why lie?

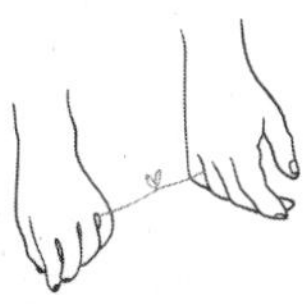

Anyway, from the first moment I saw Sushila, I liked her, and I am sure she also liked me. What was there not to like — I was tall, had a good job in a government office, and was the only son of my parents (my father was a civil engineer — so, I was considered quite a catch!) I told Sushila straightaway, that I did not want her to work after marriage. I wanted a proper, loving wife who would look after me and my parents. That is a full time job, I said to her.

She agreed... after a little hesitation. But my point is, she agreed. How was I to know her parents had given her an ultimatum? She had seen and rejected five boys by then! In our community, girls cannot reject matrimonial proposals — only boys can. Anyway, I was happy she hadn't rejected me, and the marriage date was fixed. We were very frank that way — and dowry had been discussed from the start. A middleman is needed for such delicate matters, and we had a trusted chap, known to the entire colony.

If Sushila's family did not have enough money to give us, they should have said so from the beginning. But they kept quiet — they wanted their daughter to somehow get married and save the family further dishonour. Later, I was told by Sushila that her father had had to borrow a lot of money to meet our dowry demands. That is not my fault! I told her so.

I said, 'We were getting double of what your father gave us, but since I liked you, we compromised.' That night, we had our first big fight. Sushila accused me and my family of being greedy and unreasonable. She said there were many better boys who would have been happy to marry her for free — without her father paying a single paisa.

I got angry — naturally! And told her she should have married one of them. Why did her father send the middleman to fix the alliance in that case? Sushila stopped talking to me for a week. This looked really awkward, since we all ate together, and Sushila helped my mother to cook and serve. I spoke to her after a week and asked her to forget what had happened.

She said, 'Women never forget insults.' But how had I insulted her? She started keeping to herself after that... and it was difficult to have conjugal relations with her. She was my wife! I had every right to demand what was my right! But I kept silent, not wanting to force myself on her. I am not such a bad fellow, also. After a month or so, I started to feel frustrated — you understand. And a little angry. I had married for what? To lie in my bed twiddling my thumbs at night, while my colleagues were enjoying?

This was most unfair, and I decided that night to try with Sushila, after she had washed the thaalis and cleaned the kitchen. She had stopped changing into her nightie after that big fat argument, and her clothes smelled of haldi and kothmir. I told myself to ignore all that, and try. So, I stretched my arm and caught hold of her shoulder. She shuddered and jerked her entire body to the other side of the cot. I thought she would fall on the floor. She also pushed my arm away, very rudely.

This was a big insult! Which man would be able to tolerate such a defiant act from his wife? I wanted to slap her there and then and make her see sense. This was too much! What would my parents think? That their son had become a eunuch? I showed a lot of self control and held myself back. Sushila must have felt encouraged by my weakness... and from that day she started to sleep on the floor. I was deeply hurt, and more than that, insulted. This is not how decent girls behave after marriage.

It was getting very awkward for me. Especially since I was sure my mother had sensed something was wrong. She must have seen Sushila folding up her mattress and putting it away carefully every morning. No wonder one day my mother asked out of the blue, 'When will we get some good news?' This was exactly at the time Sushila was serving me a hot chappati. Instead of placing it politely on my thaali, she dropped it on my lap. I know it was deliberately done.

Before I could reply, Sushila said a bit too loudly, 'I am not planning a baby. God only knows what will happen after this lockdown ends.' She said 'I'. Not 'we'. As if she could have a baby by herself, without involving me. I was very angry, but kept quiet.

That night I gave it to her. I said, 'Don't think too great of yourself, okay? Remember, you and your family lived in a cramped up one bhk flat in Malad. Now you live with me like a maharani, with a room and a bathroom to yourself! All this luxury without your phutka father paying a paisa to us. Okay. I will show you. Don't think I am a napusakaling — a hijra. Let's see what happens when you come to the room tonight. After brushing your teeth for ten minutes and doing what not in the toilet. Just see. I will claim my conjugal rights — right there and then. On the floor. If you try and push me off, I will raise my hand. I may also kick you — that's what you deserve, you kutti. You kuttey-kutti ki bachchi. Showing ghamand to your husband! Now you will see what the man you married is made of... oh, one more thing. My mother is already looking for a proper wife for me... someone who knows my worth. Someone whose father will willingly provide a flat and car. But for that to happen, my mother has to wait for the lockdown to be lifted. You will wake up from your trance and realise you are not the only woman in the world. You wondered aloud, "God only knows what will happen after this lockdown ends... " Let me tell you before God does — our marriage will end. '

GANPATI BAPPA MORYA

'Baba, does Ganpati Bappa know about this coronavirus? Will he come to our home this year, or avoid us? Will he also have to wear a mask?' What could I answer? I stopped what I was doing — basically nothing — and evaded a direct reply.

I answered, 'Ganpati Bappa knows everything...' My son Ameya (named after Ganeshji, our family's most beloved deity), is just seven years old. But Ameya is too smart! I am not just boasting like those showoff fathers in our colony who think their kids are all geniuses. Ameya is smart in a different way — not in class. Not at studies. Not like their children. Maybe others don't see him like that, because they don't know Ameya. He has certain problems, which his mother and I are aware of, but don't know exactly what those problems are. She is a school teacher in the nearby municipality school, where Ameya is enrolled. I work as a clerk in the Municipal Corporation.

Our life is simple. I go to work, my wife goes to work,

Ameya attends a few hours of school, then comes home to his grandmother. No complaints. My mother is not a nagging type. She is kind and good and cooks our food very nicely, with a lot of patience and love. Ganesh Utsav is our biggest festival. Bigger than Diwali, even. Ameya starts getting excited about it February onwards... and begins drawing Ganpati Bappa in his drawing books. Ameya is very good at drawing. Much ahead of other children his age. Yes, it is true, he is slow in other subjects, and sometimes he doesn't talk for days, if his mood is bad. But his mother and I know Ameya has other good qualities that other people may not understand.

He sings so nicely. Good sur, good voice. He can pick up any tune — classical, also! I listen to Bhimsen Joshi and Kishoritai from the moment I wake up. Ameya must have heard all those abhangs and raagas when he was in his mother's womb. Which is why he has no difficulty humming even a complicated raag like Khamaj.

People we have asked about children like our Ameya keep using the word 'special'. Arrey baba, we know he is special, we are his parents! But what they mean is different. What they don't say is they think he is 'abnormal'. Or 'retarded'. Which he most certainly isn't! Our Ameya is fine and precious. He was born in August — in the middle of the Ganesh Utsav — imagine! We were overjoyed and decided to call him 'Ameya', after Lord Ganesh. It had other meanings also — 'pure' and 'boundless' and 'magnanimous'. But for our small parivar, Ameya was enough... he was our little Ganeshji. He looked perfectly normal as a baby. Behaved like all the other babies in the maternity ward. How were we to know... anything? We just loved him as he was. As he is, today.

Maybe this fact, that he was born during the festival, stayed with Ameya, because he made such a big connection with God. At one point, when he was three years old, he started thinking he was Ganeshji. My mother, his mother and I do daily puja to Ganeshji in our small temple. We light a diya, once in the morning, once just after sunset. When we manage to pluck fresh hibiscus from the bush in the compound, we offer a few flowers to Ganeshji.

Ameya would tell us to do his puja also, saying, 'I am him and he is me!' Ameya knows all the Ganesh Artis and Sanskrit shlokas. He recites them with me, during worship. No other child of his age has this skill or knowledge. He can create a Ganesh moorti with clay, mud, sand, dough... any soft substance. When his Aaji kneads the atta for chappati, she always gives a ball of dough to Ameya... we know what he will make from it — Ganpati! She gives him mustard seeds or chauli for the eyes, I give him small twigs for the tusks. Within a few minutes, Ameya makes a beautiful Ganeshji... always a little different. Sometimes the trunk is to the left, sometimes to the right, sometimes it is up. I have taken many pictures of all this on my phone, even though my camera is not so good.

I show these pictures to the teachers in his school. But they take no interest and tell me, 'This is all theek hai... but who will teach him 2+2? He still doesn't know ABCD. Writes everything ulta.' Once I asked the lady teacher, 'Madam, have you ever seen any seven year old who can paint the sky like Ameya?'

She laughed at me, and said rudely, 'Painting sky won't fill his stomach later in life. How will this boy get a job, painting pictures? Which office will he join?' I felt sad, but kept quiet. Sometimes I hear Ameya talking to Ganpati Bappa, as if Bappa is a person sitting next to him. He has a full, proper conversation. I don't interfere or interrupt him. All three of us at home understand Ameya very well. Ganpati Bappa is his friend. His only friend. Because in school nobody wants to be his friend.

I heard him asking Bappa, 'Will you come to Mumbai this year? Tell me honestly... don't lie. Are you also scared of the coronavirus? It is a very bad thing, I know that. But you can come and it will get scared and run away. So please come and save us. I will make a special garland for you, better than the one I made last year. It will be my birthday... we can cut a cake together, and share modaks. Okay? Bye!'

He must have been happy with what Ganeshji told him because he was smiling away and eating all the palak bhaji up — he doesn't like eating vegetables otherwise. His mother and Aaji looked pleased as Ameya finished everything in his thali and asked me, 'When are we going to make sure our Ganpati Bappa is ready in the workshop?'

Each year, we make at least three visits to the Parel studio where most of the Ganesh moortis are made. We always book with the same kalakar, the same sculptor, year after year, because Ameya likes the way Satish Bhau painted Ganeshji's eyes. Ameya also asks Satish Bhau to paint Bappa's throne, and the mouse at Ganeshji's feet, in blue and gold colours. Satish Bhau listens to Ameya and they have become friends over time. They share their love for Bappa, that is why they get along so nicely.

This year, so far at least, we have not been able to go to the workshop because of the lockdown. It is hard to explain all this to a child, but I keep trying. His mother told him everything will open by the time Ganesh Chaturthi is celebrated. He stared at her and said, 'But I asked Ganpati Bappa yesterday, and he just kept quiet...' I also told Ameya not to worry so much. There was still time. By August everything would be much better.

See... I cannot lie. I work in the Mumbai Municipality, so I know what we are facing. Who can say what will happen by the third week of August? We are still struggling like anything to control the situation. Every day very very sad, worried and tensed up family members of Covid-19 patients are coming and complaining. They are saying, 'Will our father die like a dog in these dirty, filthy wards? So many people are dying and you people are lying and saying, "They are alive... they are alive." Some bodies are thrown into gutters. Some are taken away just like that and cremated. All this is not good. It is a "paap".'

The numbers are going up and up. Doctors are fully fed up! Nurses have gone back to Kerala. Sometimes, even the ward boys stay away. Conditions are very bad... but we cannot say that openly. This ward and that ward... they are saying bring this into containment zone, take that out of containment zone. Clean the garbage on the road. Make the beaches safaa safaa. How we can do all this! Public should also think and understand our difficulties. See... Mumbai is too big. And we are too small. Nowadays we are stuck at home and all that. No trains. No buses. Nobody on the roads. No people. No traffic. No noise. Nothing! But Ganesh Chaturthi celebrations can never stop — lockdown or no lockdown. I told Ameya not to worry.

I requested his mother to distract him. She was also very tired, with no clear future in sight. Her classes and exams are in disarray. There is no proper communication and co-ordination. It was a good thing she was just a junior teacher, taking lessons for fourth and fifth standards. Some of her colleagues in higher classes were complaining non-stop and saying there was no hope for their students getting into college. Ameya hears all these conversations and starts laughing.

He says, 'See... I told you... school and college is all bekaar. I want to stay at home and play catch-catch with my Bappa.' His mother has done a lot of research on why Ameya is so different. She said he will remain like this only, forever. There is no treatment as such. But she also said many great people in the world were born like this. And they still managed to come up in life like anything. I also feel confident that Ganeshji will protect our Ameya. That is why, no matter what happens, I still take the boy to see Lalbaugh Chha Raja every year and place his head on Ganeshji's feet. It is one ritual I perform without fail. For Ameya, too, this is the biggest moment... the darshan!

He doesn't sleep the previous night, and keeps asking, 'Shall we go? Shall we go? Ganpati Bappa is waiting for me... Bappa is saying, "Come soon, come soon".'

I had never ever disappointed Ameya. We would leave for the pandal in Lalbaugh, after taking tea and eating poha. By the time we reached, there would already be a huge crowd — baap re! Devotees from all over come and take their place in the queue from the previous night.

Thousands and thousands of people visit the Raja, for that brief darshan. See... it is about belief. Raja always blesses those who come to him with a pure heart. Ameya has the purest heart — that much I know. And so strong is Ameya's love for his Bappa, he refuses to see the visarjan. Forget about travelling to Girgaum Chowpatty to say goodbye to all the Sarvajanik and family Ganpatis who stay on earth for ten days, only to go back to their Mother by allowing devotees to immerse them in the sea, Ameya does not let us watch this beautiful and sentimental and touching ceremony even on TV. He gets furious and starts throwing things everywhere — anything that he finds — could be glasses or thaalis or even a wooden table lamp. He shouts, 'Bappa... don't go! Don't leave me!' After that drama gets over, he cries and cries. Ameya does not like goodbyes at all.

But this year it is a different story. We have to worry about Covid-19. How would the crowds be managed? Who can control worshippers? I was feeling nervous. Even with masks and all that, who was to know which person has it, who doesn't and all that. But how could I tell all these things to Ameya?

He would stop eating — this much I can say for sure. Then his mother and my mother will pounce on me for upsetting Ameya.

I tried to hint at the problem, saying lightly, 'Oh... this coronavirus is creating big problems for everybody this year. So many requests are coming to the office from Sarvajanik pandal people asking our help for proper bandobast. Police wallas also saying, we can't control. Social distancing makes no sense when thousands gather to offer prayers. How to say "no" also?'

Before I could continue, I heard Ameya let out a piercing scream. He rushed to our small little home shrine and complained loudly against me to Ganeshji. Nothing could console my boy. I felt very bad also. It is nobody's fault that this has happened. Who knew last year that there would be so much gadbad in the world? When we went to pay our respects to Ganpati Bappa at Lalbaugh, we also shouted and joined the chorus, 'Ganpati Bappa Morya... Pudhchha Varshi Lavkar Ya...'

Ameya danced and sang in the gully, ate prasad, came home happy, wearing his new clothes. That night he painted a very large Ganeshji with the colours in the paint box I had given him. This time, Ameya had chosen to paint on the inside of our front door, explaining, 'Bappa said he wants to keep an eye on us... in case we are being naughty!'

Mumbai and Ganesh Utsav... the whole city waits for those ten days. Ameya is confident nothing will stop Ganeshji from visiting our city. He said, 'Ganpati Bappa is stronger and bigger and greater than this corona. He told me just now, he will come and drive out that horrible, ugly, mean monster. Tell your office... our Raja is on his way.'

LOCKDOWN FUNERAL

'This side... this side... ladies, this side please.' There was no need for the priest to intervene in such a crude way. After all, we were only eighteen people at the funeral. We were there to say our final farewell to 'M' – the man I had been married to for thirty-two years... till.... well. What's the point of that 'till'. He was dead. The police had said no more than 20 people at this electric crematorium near the sea — my first time at a crematorium, electric or otherwise. Our religious practices were different, you see. But let me not go into that. Even though 'M' had not died of Covid-19, and could have followed our faith, he had left instructions about his last rites as soon as he knew the end was close.

Besides... we had not spoken to each other in 22 years. Not exchanged a single word! Not even when our beloved son got married. Then our lovely daughter. 'M' had left me by then. Just like that. Left! For that one. I never used her name. 'That one' was good enough. I had not seen her after 'M' walked away that awful afternoon, when the three of us sat in the living

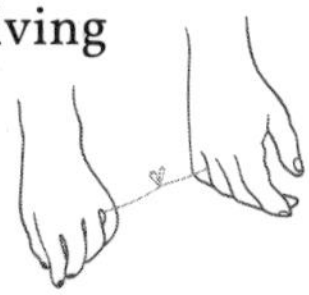

room of what was 'our' home — mine and 'M's'. The children were visiting their grandmother. And our staff knew when to disappear. 'M' had come to plead for a divorce. And brought 'That One' with him.

Why??? I had screamed and almost pushed her out of the front door. 'M' had stood like a shield in front of her — and told me to step aside, so they could come in. What could I have done? I had let loose my tongue and called her names, called him names. Obviously! I had pointed to the painting on the wall — our portrait! Painted by an English portraitist of renown.

'See this...' I had shouted. Then pointed to another portrait, of 'M' and me and the two children, when they were toddlers. This one was painted by one of India's greatest artists.

'You are breaking up our beautiful family... our beautiful life. Have you no shame? What sort of a woman are you?' I had said, my green-brown cat eyes flashing, as I gathered my silk flowing caftan around my slim body and stuck out my breasts, allowing cleavage to peep through the deep neckline. I wanted her to see what 'M' had seen in me for all these years. I was a beauty! Admired by society and respected for my lineage. I had my position, money, talent and looks — the very reasons that had made 'M' pursue me till I said 'yes'. Granted, 'M' came from an even wealthier family. And his lineage was impeccable, too. And what was 'That One'?

A nothing! A nobody. No family background, no legacy, and frankly, no looks. She was what we called 'common'. 'M' was such a snob! What had he seen in her? I was baffled and livid! 'M' and I represented the upper crust in our small community. We were *the* couple, envied and admired by all. Our homes, cars, art, soirees... yes — we had it all! 'That One' was an upstart. No background to speak of. And he had fallen for her. What did she have to hold a man of such taste and refinement?

Just to give you a small but significant example, 'M' liked me in pearls. 'That One' preferred diamonds — the bigger the better. You know... the kind NRI women wear to impress other NRI women. I found that vulgar. At our home, 'M' liked Western style dinners, three or four courses, a change of service, silver flatware, English crockery... that sort of thing. He enjoyed Bread and Butter pudding, Crème Brûlée... maybe a little Cointreau, a puff or two of his favourite Cuban.

'That One' was more a butter chicken type, who probably served gajjar halwa for dessert. What can I say? I still don't understand what 'M' saw in her. How could they have attended concerts together? Could she even pronounce 'concerto' or know what it was? Freddy, our knowledgeable, music loving friend, used to stay with us in our London home, and we always hosted a dinner for him and his lovely wife when they came to Mumbai. 'That One' didn't go beyond balle balle, bhangra and at the most some ghazals!

I was horrified when a friend of ours from London sent me a video of 'M' dancing with her at some hideous sangeet, with everybody wearing the most garish ethnic clothes. I couldn't get over 'M' dressed like a band master in some embroidered ethnic outfit, with a shiny stole draped over his shoulders! This man, who wore a black tie like a proper English aristocrat, was making an idiot of himself shaking his hips to trashy Bollywood songs! I was so embarrassed.

Of course, I did send it to our children – they needed to know how ridiculously their father was behaving. Had he gone completely mad? They surprised me by saying, 'But Ma, doesn't Dad look happy?' What on earth did they mean? Is that called 'happiness'? He didn't look happy, he looked drunk! And he was behaving like a complete idiot.

After 'M' fell seriously ill in London, I never really ran into them, nor did I want to keep in touch. I heard she was in charge of everything and was making all the appointments with top Harley Street doctors and all that. Good for her. At least she was paying back for her luxurious life by behaving like his nursemaid. The children kept going to London to visit him. Of course, they could not avoid meeting 'That One' when they met their father. But my children have been raised very well by me – they remained polite and courteous to her so as not to upset their dearly beloved father. Initially, I would bombard them with questions about her and ask how it was working out between 'M' and that whole set up. Then, I realised my children did not want to discuss all that. So, I stopped.

It was only when 'M' decided to move back to India and into a palatial penthouse, that I started feeling awkward. After all,

Mumbai maybe a huge city, but socially, there are only a few old families that count. Like ours. We meet the same set all the time — at the club or over dinners and lunches. Or at the races. And of course, during art and charity auctions. 'That One' was a complete misfit in our circle. She was so dreadfully gauche. While they lived in London, I was okay with it. This was a bit too close for me to pretend I didn't care! Mind you, it wasn't about the divorce settlement, or the heirloom jewellery or cash or anything like that. 'M' had been more than fair and given me whatever I had demanded... and more. The children had been settled as well. So, it wasn't about material comforts. It was the acute embarrassment of running into them somewhere. Because of that fear, I stopped going out.

My children used to meet both of them quite often and they kept their meetings from me. Silly things! I would find out from the old cook who now worked for them. And 'M's' old driver, whose son works for me. The jeweller would also tell me what 'That One' had ordered — and we would laugh at her taste! She didn't belong to our world at all. And that's what bothered me the most.

Oh well... when 'M' fell ill in Mumbai, I felt a little bad and would have liked to visit him in hospital. But I stopped myself. I couldn't stand the thought of running into 'That One'. She was there all the time. I heard she barely went home to change and then, she'd be right back to maintain her vigil by 'M's' bedside. If she left him even for an hour, he would start asking for her, summoning the nurses and making a big fuss. Not once did he utter my name or ask for me! The children said 'M' was looking very frail and had shrunk to half his size. Frankly, I wanted to go and sit next to him, and sing his favourite arias, or play his most loved symphonies… something 'That One' couldn't possibly do or understand.

He used to enjoy my singing, even though mine was not a trained voice. I was no Callas — I know that! 'M' used to say I sang like Celine Dion… and even looked a bit like her. Such a flatterer! He could certainly belt out Frank Sinatra and Dean Martin numbers…and boy! The two of us jiving on the dance floor used to pull in an audience. I would have liked to dance just for him. Yes! Right there around his hospital bed. Just to remind him of happier times. Or take profiteroles… a big slice of pineapple cream cake… Bohri style mutton samosas… asparagus mousse… I knew 'M's palate. But that was out of the question with her around, guarding him like a hawk. I suppose she must have loved him in her own way. I did feel very jealous of their togetherness, especially during the lockdown — I had never felt this isolated and alone in our beautiful home. Even though 'M' was in and out of ICU, at least he had her by his side. And our loving children, who looked after him so well.

And then came the news he had slipped away. It was the 70th day of the lockdown. And Mumbai was still closed. All those checks and nakabandis with police stopping cars and asking nosy questions were still going on and on. I was as fed up as everyone else. When my son called to say 'M' had passed, I sighed and said nothing at all. There was nothing to say. But everything to feel. I disconnected and asked for green tea. I stroked my cat and stared at our wedding photograph.

How young and happy and gorgeous we looked! I didn't feel sad... I felt empty. And a little numb. I looked at my chipped nail polish and smiled — 'M' was very particular about well-manicured nails.

I didn't have nail polish remover in my bathroom closet. And the shops were still closed. I walked across to the large silver-framed mirror in the ante-room — this was our favourite spot for aperitifs before dinner. We would listen to Chopin, chat about a play we had enjoyed, or laugh at our relatives, before heading to the dining room. It was one ritual I missed. We made a good couple. A handsome couple. Admired and adored by many. Well... such is life, I thought, as my beautiful Persian with large geen eyes, purred and arched his back.

'M' had planned his funeral well. I was mentally prepared and all that. My children had applied for the appropriate permissions and we were told to assemble at the crematorium by 5 p.m. I wanted to look dignified, regal and beautiful. 'M' liked me in blue. I had kept the ice blue chiffon with a matching blouse pressed and ready for weeks. I would be wearing the Basra pearls 'M' had gifted me on our fifth anniversary, and our engagement ring, of course. Perhaps, I would skip the pearl and diamond bracelet, but definitely wear the vintage platinum Patek Phillipe we had acquired at an auction in Hong Kong. Lipstick, for sure! 'M' liked me wearing a particular Lancome red. He said it suited my complexion. My hair was at its worst! The soft perm had grown out, the mahogany colour had faded, and the highlights resembled nasty errors committed by a child with a paintbrush. I was looking my worst! Not joking. I was dreading to see what 'That One' would show up in. And I was, for the first time in my life, feeling diffident. What if her nails were perfectly painted? Her hair, trimmed and styled with no roots showing? What if she had been gymming all through 'M's' illness and her body was in great shape? What if she had planned her outfit as much for him as for us? Would she wear his favourite shade of ice blue and overshadow me? I debated which shades to place on my head as I arrived... 'M' loved the tortoise shell Balenciagas. What if he had given her a similar pair and she decided to sport it? Oh... and the handbag... I was going to carry my old Chanel or Lady Dior. She would no doubt flash an LV or a gaudy Fendi. No heels, of course. We would all have to remove our footwear for the final goodbye. Did she have the good sense to do the same?

The florists were shut. There was just no beauty, no dignity left in a Lockdown Funeral, was there? I would have ordered tokris and tokris of fragrant mogras — 'M' loved jasmines, and they were in season. I would have sourced tiger lilies and long-stemmed white roses, and draped his body in his favourite old Jamevar shawl. 'M' was such a bon vivant — I would have made sure he left the world in the grand style he had lived his life. It was no longer in my hands. How sad.

Driving five odd kilometres in our adored Jag — the silver grey mark VII — I stared at Mumbai's deserted streets. My heart was as stripped of emotions as the roads were of crowds. I looked out at the sea as we drove past Marine Drive — no lovers sitting on the parapet. Mumbai had no love left anymore. 'M' had died. Hundreds of people were dying everywhere... Mumbai itself was dying. Why blame just the virus. Something much worse was corroding everything... hate! At that awful moment, I was filled with dread... would 'That One' spot me before I spotted her? I swept in, my head held high, just as I had rehearsed a hundred times at home, before the full-length mirror on my Burma teak almirah... It still bore 'M's' aftershave fragrance... heaven knows how. Or maybe, my nostrils held its memory. I spotted a few familiar faces — 'M's' doctor, his staff, my children, a couple of what I called 'oldie-goldies'... in my mind, they had grown old, not me.

I still couldn't spot her! Had she decided it was wiser and more discreet to stay away? I looked quizzically at my daughter, and she averted my gaze. Standing next to her, and being held in a light embrace, was a tiny, shrunken bag of bones — bent over with grief, and hardly able to look up. She was dressed in what we would call 'home clothes' — an unironed cotton caftan with block print. Her hair was in an untidy bun, with strands of fading grey framing a thin face. She was wearing bifocals much too large for her thin face. Her skin was spotted and she wore no make-up. I guessed it was her, when I recognised 'M's old watch on her emaciated wrist — the sturdy Daytona. 'M' called it a 'workhorse' and preferred it to some of his far more expensive, complicated watches. Why would this woman be wearing his watch... unless... unless...

In that one brief moment, I was freed. I went and took my place on the other side of my daughter. The three women in 'M's' life were together in grief. Finally, it was all over.

A WHIFF OF ETERNITY

I have to be honest — I mean, I could die of Covid-19 tomorrow! What's the point in lying at this stage? I could die. You could die. We could all die. The thing about this little shit of a microbe is that it spares nobody. The scary corona thing — the bloody pandemic — has made non-liars out of all those of us who wasted so many years pretending, pretending, pretending. I had decided to stop lying and pretending. I liked girls, not boys. Okay? You have a problem with that? Go fuck yourself. No more hiding and playing games.

Had Minu been wearing any other perfume but THAT one when our eyes met on the jogging track near home, I am sure I would have stayed away from her. I mean... all I had seen were her eyes above that heavy duty mask covering most of her face! As I jogged past this mysterious woman's taut and fit form, gloves and all, I got a whiff of 'Eternity' — the one fragrance in the world I had sworn I would never allow myself to react to — not after my break-up. Not ever! Like jilted lovers block out sentimental conversations, voices, notes, gifts,

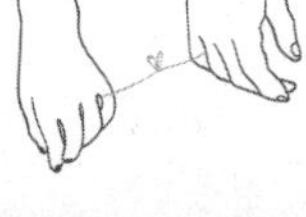

touches, I had blocked out a particular fragrance.

But that was two years ago. My nose was sensitive and active again. I was sniffing and smelling with enthusiasm. But 'Eternity' still hurt. It continued to haunt. I had broken several other promises made to myself during that difficult period. I had changed cities, quit a great job in Delhi, found a lousy new one in Chandigarh and now... here I was, back in Mumbai with my tail between my legs.

Imagine! I was forced to come 'home' to live with my parents after a break of seven years. Heartbreak had extracted its price. I was determined to start on a fresh, uncomplicated note this time. I couldn't afford to screw up. My parents were not overjoyed to have their single, unmarried and now overweight daughter back in their smallish flat in Dadar colony. But they weren't that cruel either to not let me back into their simple, retired, professorial lives.

Just as I was settling into this unexpected new life, wondering what the fuck to do next, the world turned topsy turvy and Narendra Modi announced the fucking national lockdown. We were given four hours to deal with the devastating news that was going to change our lives forever. Four hours! Initially, I didn't get it! What? A microbe in China was screwing the world? Rubbish! We were overreacting – what sort of nonsense is this? A bat in Wuhan had more power than a nuclear bomb! I ignored the news.

But my parents kept saying, 'Very contagious, very contagious... don't step outside, wash your hands, drink hot water, gargle with salt.' I laughed and pretended to be busy. My office had announced WFH (work from home), I was in a brand new job, an alien set up, I had to earn that desperately needed salary. It was half of what I was getting in Delhi. But what the hell, I was lucky to have a job at all! And no rent to pay.

The worst part of being back in the home I had fled years ago was the new lockdown regime because the part-time servants could no longer come to the flat since our building fell in the 'red zone' and all the flat owners had decided to bar outsiders from entering the premises. This was terrible! There was nobody to clean the place, and help Aie with the cooking. This meant just one thing — I had to do it! Aie had a problem with her back, and Baba had never entered the kitchen or lifted a duster in his life.

Housework didn't bother me — I was used to doing it in Delhi. But that was different. My partner Roohi was there to share the work, and just having her in the same room made me forget I was slaving. Coming home after a long day and knowing Roohi was already back from her design atelier waiting for me... oh... bliss, bliss, bliss! I would breathe in the air deeply while opening the latch on the gate. I would wait for 'that' moment — a whiff of 'Eternity' would alert my nostrils — she was there! Upstairs! Waiting for me to rush up and hold her in my arms. I would take the two flight of stairs and grab Roohi in a tight embrace before getting down to organising dinner for the two of us.

Roohi was the romantic one. She would light aroma candles, get Alexa to play 'our' songs, and sip her favourite white wine, while I quickly chopped veggies for the salad and put daal and rice into the pressure cooker. She would offer to lay the table, but I would insist on doing it myself. Just watching Roohi in a silk kimono, relaxed and smiling, was enough of a stress buster for me. Looking back on our last terrible fight, I feel relieved it led to my ending the relationship even though I thought I would die without Roohi in my life.

I didn't die-die. But I did die on many levels. I tried living in the same place and staying on in the same job for two years. Nothing was working. I was seeing a therapist who had put me on a course of anti-depressant pills. The side effects of those were leading to other issues — weight gain and sluggishness. Something snapped around the end of February, and I quit. I needed to get the fuck out of Delhi. But without a decent income, I would not be able to afford the rent or pay my bills. I was used to a certain lifestyle — not lavish, mind you, but comfortable. You know, weekends spent loafing about and eating at new places in Cyber Hub, drinking at new watering holes, buying Roohi gifts at DLF Select Citywalk. Standard stuff.

But my timing to make all these major changes really sucked. There were no jobs, as more and more media offices were scaling back and firing long time staff, right and left. Mumbai was the only realistic option. My parents didn't sound enthusiastic, but they realized I was in a mess — emotionally and financially. I had given a lot of money from my savings to Roohi — strictly as a loan. But I also knew I had kissed the money goodbye and it would never be returned! That was not the difficult part. It was when I shut my heart's door on Roohi, memories, longing, Delhi, 'Eternity', booked a train ticket to Mumbai, that my destiny changed.

The lockdown changed everything! I got here in March... a day before India shut shop. When I look back, I thank my stars I bought the train ticket on that particular day or else I would have been stuck in Delhi, without a job, without Roohi, without a future, without hope, without any life. Once Roohi walked out, so did most of 'our' friends. I had never felt this isolated and unwanted. Nobody phoned. I stopped meeting people or making social plans. Here in Mumbai, with Aie and Baba around, I did not feel as suicidal or alone, even though we rarely chatted or laughed or shared pleasantries. They read books on history and sociology. I pretended to be busy. Thank God they had finally stopped asking me, 'Have you met a nice boy?' And when nosy neighbourhood Mauvshis called to ask, 'Has Shaalu set the date? No? Hurry up! Hurry up! All the good boys in the community are already booked.' Like 'good boys' were flats in Panvel which my parents could book in advance. I detested this life. It was only that short respite in the park, my evening walk, which made me feel there would be a silver lining to those early monsoon clouds racing across Mumbai skies.

Her eyes were kind and smiling. I nodded to let her know I recognised her. It doesn't look good to appear too pushy. She slowed down her jogging pace, and kept running on the spot, to allow me to catch up. I felt embarrassed, because I was already out of breath, huffing and puffing. Sweating profusely, as well!

'You are new here... I mean, to the park, this area...' she said, her voice muffled behind her beautiful mask (hmm, a handstiched denim one, I noted). I pointed to my building and said, 'Decided to spend time with my parents... you know... lockdown duty!' I made it sound cool. Like a semi-joke.

Her eyes smiled some more. She wore mascara, and her eyes were lined with a green pencil. It was impossible to figure out her age, but going by her figure and the fading highlights in her hair (which was tied in a high pony), I guessed we were the same age — mid-thirties. I could recognise the dangerous signs welling up within — the Roohiwala signs. My voice had changed. And I was flirting with my large, expressive eyes, staring openly at the lovely stranger.

'Shaalu...' I said, and tried a gloved fist greeting. Her hands remained where they were. 'Minu...' she replied, adding, 'our names rhyme.'

We both laughed. 'Do you know where to source jowar ka atta from? I am new to the area, and avoid wheat. Gluten-resistant.'

I said a bit too eagerly, 'I can run home and get you bajra. My mother makes bajra bhakris... can get you those, too.'

Minu's eyes smiled, 'You are so sweet and helpful and kind... it's hard to make friends in Mumbai.'

My heart was hers. I wanted to tear open my chest and hand it to her, there and then while she ran on the spot and I panted. 'I have run out of too many essentials... and my grocery store is saying to stock up with whatever they have before even those supplies run out. How are you managing?'

I shrugged and said, 'My folks are old timers. They have a good relationship with the kiraanawalla. You just give me your list... I will arrange whatever you want. Except booze! But I have an extra bottle of decent gin.'

Her eyes were shining! Minu was pleased with me! She said, 'Let's punch in our numbers when we finish this round. It will be easier to co-ordinate everything from now on.'

Oh my God! She had said, 'From now on.' I wanted to jump in the air and yell, 'Yayyyyy!' But stopped myself.

She said, 'Gotta get going... Zoom party in twenty minutes! Must tart up!' My heart sank. Zoom party! With whom? And why tart up? She could have asked me to join after we exchanged numbers. But she hadn't. I couldn't sleep all night thinking of Minu partying with very successful, very glamorous people — she must be a highly sought after person, why would she befriend me?

The next day was awful for me, Aie had woken up with a slight temperature and a sore throat. Baba was worried, and wanted me to take her to the nearest testing centre in the evening.

I said, 'No! That won't be possible!' before I could stop myself. Baba looked upset and angry, asking agitatedly, 'Why not?'

Like a fool I blurted out, 'I have to give a packet of jowar and three avocadoes to my friend in the park.' He looked at me like I had gone mad. 'You want your mother to die of Covid while you run to give fruits and vegetables to some friend?'

'Baba – not fruits and vegetables. Jowar and avocadoes – there's a big difference.' He looked like his eyes would fall out of his sockets .Then his body slumped. With a wave of his hand and in a tired, small voice he said, 'Go… go to your friend. I will take care of Aie.'

I am ashamed to admit I did just that. Since there was still a small window left for people to buy essentials, I all but ran to the corner store and pleaded with the owner to give me the atta. He asked, 'Will bajra do?' He was out of jowar… shit! Bastard! I took the bajra anyway and went in search of avocadoes. No luck. So I spent on imported 'Beauty pears' instead. And bought three, top grade, organically grown Hapus mangoes, hand-picked from the vendor's peti.

I placed everything in a jute bag and went in search of Minu. She was talking on her cell phone (latest model) and waved out. I lifted up the jute bag and indicated with a thumbs up sign that I had succeeded in my mission. As I walked up to her, following my nose, she turned her back to me and continued talking in a low voice. I didn't feel bad or anything. Must have been an important work call.

Her mood had changed when she abruptly ended the call. 'Let's run,' she said, ignoring my outstretched hand holding the jute bag. I loved her workout gear and complimented her. She kept running like she hadn't heard me.

When we completed ten rounds of the small park, she sat down on a wooden bench and pointed to a space three feet away for me to sit.

'Something wrong?' I asked.

'Just a shitty day at work,' she replied.

After a pause I asked, 'What do you do?'

Minu said, 'I am a stylist... you know? I style Bollywood stars... models... celebrities. But because of this fucking lockdown, no work is happening. All shoots are cancelled. Most glam magazines have shut down or are using file photos. I don't know how I am going to pay my credit card bills this month. And I have an EMI on hold — for this fucking fancy phone that I no longer need.'

I was so impressed. No wonder she was so stylish — she was a stylist! Even her mask was stylish, glittering away with tiny sequins. I was thinking of ways to make her smile.

So I blurted out, 'I can give you money — not much. But what I can spare. You can return it after the lockdown.' She smiled!

Her eye make-up was of a deep plum colour and it suited her eyes. 'Really? You have money to give? I love youuuuuuuu.'

My heart stopped beating. My lungs also collapsed. I wasn't breathing. She didn't notice. She was talking on the phone animatedly and telling someone she had managed to 'score some funds'. Meanwhile, I was asking myself where I'd get the money from. Nothing else mattered.

'How much can you spare, bro?' she asked. Why was she calling me bro?

I didn't reply immediately, so she held up her index finger. 'One thousand?' I asked. She burst out laughing, 'Dude… what does anybody get for 1K… come on, talk sense.'

I felt so foolish! So I added, 'Arrey… I was just joking! I guess you need one lakh, right?'

She nodded, 'To start with. That will just about cover some small stuff.'

I swore to myself I would get it for her. Then I heard her on the phone again. She was discussing the colour of a lehenga and talking about the embroidery style on the achkan.

Wow! Maybe she was in charge of styling someone really famous – a big, big Bollywood star. Maybe she was styling Alia for her wedding. I asked eagerly if she was Alia's personal stylist. She said vaguely, 'Sort of. She is one of our clients.'

'Have you met her? Interacted with her directly? Is she a sweet person?' Minu smiled. Again! Picked up her water bottle and announced, 'Gotta run! Another fucking Zoom thingie. Webinar... such a waste of time. So much bakwas. See you tomorrow, bro. Bring cash, okay?'

She was gone. Leaving a trail of 'Eternity'. Minu had left the jute bag with the bajra atta and the pears. Poor thing, she had forgotten to take it from me in her hurry. I'd make sure she took it with her tomorrow — the atta, pears... and cash. I would pack the money separately, of course. When I got home, Aie and Baba had left for the clinic. There was a short note on the kitchen table. Baba hated cell phones. And Aie was feeling weak, so maybe she hadn't called for that reason. Aie had left food for me, near the gas range.

But I wanted cash, not food. And I found it inside Baba's steel trunk, in a brown paper envelope neatly labelled, 'Emergency fund For Medical Expenses. Rupees Three lakhs.' Baba had always been a very organised, disciplined man. Inside were old notes, neatly folded. I counted them carefully — two lakhs fifty thousand. He must have removed fifty thousand when he took Aie for a check up. I was honest enough to take only one lakh for Minu. I could have taken the balance. But Minu had asked for one lakh only. I kept the money under my pillow and tried to sleep. By the time I heard sounds in the kitchen, it was well past midnight. It was Baba. Just Baba.

'Where's Aie?' I asked sleepily.

'At Kasturba Hospital,' he replied. 'Aie's test results will come tomorrow... if she tests positive...' Baba touched his forehead and looked skywards. My heart sank. Not for Aie. But for myself.

Khalaas! I was doomed. This meant just one thing — Baba and I would be in quarantine and I wouldn't be able to leave the house or give the money to Minu. In just a few hours, the BMC people would be here to seal not just our home, but our small building. They would sanitise everything and spray all the rooms, as they kept showing on TV. Our wrists would be stamped and we would be told to not step outside our front door. I would be finally, hopelessly trapped.

And that was when I realised. I was trapped already. I had been trapped for a while now. Perhaps since I lost Roohi. But it was time to get out. I knew I would lose Minu. I knew it. But that was alright. I went to my room and picked up the half-used bottle of 'Eternity' — why did I still have it even — and threw it into the garbage can. I would have to figure out a way to put the money back into Baba's trunk. He was going to need it now. Baba shuffled up to where I was seated, slumped on my bed. He handed me a bottle of sanitizer. 'Aie sent it for you,' he said. And walked out.

Feeling trapped was going to be my 'new normal' from now on. If not Minu, I would find a Tinu. And I knew then itself that my future was going to be another, even bigger trap. With Baba. Aie was not coming back. And Baba couldn't live on his own.

MISS LA DI DA

'Hey!' I didn't know what to say to her after that. She stared at me in such a hostile way while I stood there, at the head of the small garden, wondering what I had done to offend Miss La Di Da. Our kids were friends, okay? We were neighbours... sort of. I mean, we weren't neighbours-neighbours in the old sense of having grown up together in the same complex or anything. Our kids went to the same school. We were all fucked with the home schooling shit. I needed help, man! Why would she behave like this? Goddess syndrome, or what? Glaring and ignoring me, like I was a turd she didn't want to step on.

Gawwwwd! These bloody women! I had met a few of her type during those boring and pointless PTAs. I hated meeting my boy's teachers and listening to the same old shit about his inattention in class. Okayyyy, that's why he is in your fancy, pricey school! You deal with it, na? But this Miss La Di Da was giving me serious grief, I tell you. Why? What the hell, man — the bachchas played in the sand pit together, they shared tricycles and balls, their nannies were besties, and the snacks from my kitchen were far more imaginative than those banana chips and roasted peanuts she packed for her sweeties — two lovely little girls, who had inherited their mother's aquiline good looks, but mercifully, not her imperious temperament.

I was back in my old bachpan ka home to take care of my parents during the lockdown. It was just me and my boy, plus his nanny. And my folks with their staff. As a single father, living with other people, even my own parents, was going to extract a huge price. I was not used to hanging with anybody these days. I preferred to be alone, with my music, poker, telescope, books. I watched old movies and kept going back to Bresson. This was my chosen world... after... never mind after what. I was not ready to accept the 'new normal', because frankly, nobody knew what the hell it was! All that big talk and those fake posts — rubbish. Everything these days was abnormal if you ask me. Maybe this snooty chica was also abnormal. The thing is, had she been a little nice, we could have helped each other with the home schooling shit.

And then, there were my parents. But I had not factored in this crazy development, okay? The last time I had lived with my folks was over 20 years ago. This was awkward! But, they had nobody else to turn to — my sister lived in New York, and she was dealing with her own Covid-19 shit there. My parents were sweet people — benign drunks who minded their own business and played bridge for relaxation. Now, without their regular foursome, they were getting on each other's nerves. And I didn't want to play umpire. I was dealing with my own shit. The mother of my child had upped and left all of a sudden

— destination unknown. She had left a poem behind. That's it. A shitty little poem about her quest for inner peace. Horseshit! I guessed she had met a like-minded cokehead during her Rishikesh retreat and decided to hang there with him for as long as the powder lasted.

After that? Who the fuck cares. She was gone. Leaving our baba in my care. She always used to say witheringly, 'Isn't it time you manned up and took some responsibility? The sperm is all yours, you know.' So it was! So it was! I remember making our baba in Goa... right there on the sand. We were both stoned out of our skulls, the sea was crashing at our feet, and for the past week, the sex had been amazing. Our baba was created in that happy zone... which had lasted for a surprisingly long period, given our wild and wonderful, totally untamed life, which was so erratic at that point, I am still in shock at some of the stuff we did. And we did one hell of a lot of stuff, I can tell you!

But now... it was a different story, right? I had majorly cleaned up my shit. I was clean, man! I had to take care of the old man — my grumpy dad was going to be 75, had a whole bunch of chronic ailments, and enough medical files to build a mini Qutb Minar in the compound. The old girl was not that much healthier. Both had what were referred to as 'co-morbidities' — the usual crap that comes with old age — hyper tension, diabetes and God knows what else. I was not an indifferent son. I loved my folks and all that. But I had been through a lot — failed marriage and a business that went south after a great start.

My old man was generous and kind... and I was not really worried about the future. He had bailed me out — or else — man, all those bounced cheques? I'd have spent the best years of my life behind bars. Instead, I decided to invest in a shrink, after I got sorted by Dad. We had our family trusts, investments... this great home, my own fabulous apartment, homes in Mahabaleshwar and Pune. I was pretty much set. My little baba was a sweet chappie... we were getting to know each other during this fucking lockdown shit. There was no option — I was stuck doing that rubbish home schooling thing with him! Imagine! Me and home schooling a kid I barely knew!

His nanny took care of everything else — I didn't have to wash his bum, or anything. But how could she cope with home school when she'd barely been to school herself? She was one of those great, hard-working nannies from Jharkhand. My little chap loved her to death. I often felt he loved her more than he loved his mother. Or me. But Kanti could not help with this new routine. And I definitely required proper help with all those bloody work sheets and assignments. That snobby Miss La Di Da was being such a bitch! What did she think? All I needed was a few minutes to figure out the kid's time table and then I would take it from there. Her little girls were eager to help — but not her! Such a tight ass — with her fancy gym clothes and head gear. It was yoga this and yoga that... like there was nothing more to life than attending yoga classes online and eating ragi cookies. Her husband was a decent fellow. What was her problem? Always glaring and scowling at me, like I was upsetting her equilibrium in some way.

Anyway, since I had loads of free time, once I was done with that school shit, I used to play bat-ball with the baba in the small common area we were permitted to use, when the lockdown rules were relaxed a bit. Miss La Di Da started complaining that my loud voice was getting on her nerves, even though her girls were cheering me. I mentioned it to my mother while enjoying a cuppa in the balcony outside my room — the one baba and I shared, as he gobbled up his freshly baked mini cheese quiche and I ate those mummywala special chicken salad sandwiches. When I cribbed about that creature who threw attitude at me for nothing, mummyji smiled and said, 'You must get her on your side, so that the children can play together a little more freely and you can get help with the homework — I hear she used to be a school teacher before she married that nice man.' For once the old lady had come up with a good idea.

The next time I ran into Miss La Di Da, I offered to help her carry the gas cylinder to her flat. These days our hyper paranoid security guys did not allow delivery of those monstrous cylinders to our homes, since someone somewhere had tested positive after the gas cylinder wala entered the kitchen. She was wearing a really attractive mask made out of some fancy organic fabric. Her hair was piled on top of her head in a top knot, and she had smudged kaajal in her eyes. All these details I could take in quickly, because my ex-wife used to work with a fashion magazine and was forever discussing this shit over the phone. Miss La Di Da was struggling with the cylinder, and her right wrist must have been hurting because she was wearing a thick, black support brace. She first pretended she didn't need my assistance, and then relented when her wrist hurt and she winced in pain.

I felt this cylinder thing was a bit too much in this complex – what sort of crazy restrictions were these? There were senior citizens staying here, with no live-in help. Who would carry their cylinders? We reached her kitchen door and the girls squealed with delight when they saw me. Her husband was around, watching CNN. He looked up, smiled and invited me in for a beer. The girls dragged me into the house and insisted I stay. I wondered why he hadn't helped with the cylinder. He looked able bodied and young.

My expression must have given me away. There was an awkward silence in the large living room, next to the neat open-style kitchen. I felt really stupid – like I had dropped a huge brick. Oh shit! There goes my chance to share homework and work sheets – that was my first, entirely selfish thought. The worst thing about the bloody lockdown had been the home schooling crap – it was so much crap! What could these little children possibly 'learn', after being forcibly seated in front of the Ipad? Their attention spans were way too small… I felt bad for the teachers, too. Imagine 'teaching' kids virtually! Imagine getting up early, preparing all those lessons and sitting in front of a screen! I was a dud at all this. A total dud. I had never bothered with baba's lessons or school assignments. It was not my department, man! I had no idea about his books or how many crayons kids required for art class. This was beginning to get to me!

I had to fucking wake up at 7 a.m., to make sure baba was ready to sit in front of that screen by 8 a.m. His school insisted on a parent sitting through the lessons and supervising homework. The kids had to be bathed and fed before classes began. This was insane! Totally insane! Some of the other parents had it much worse. They were stuck at home minus staff. Moms had to cook and clean and hang around for the class. Some of them were full-time working moms and dads adhering to the WFH schedule. Most dads preferred to leave it to moms to keep this junk going. I was totally screwed!

I desperately needed a little neighbourly help — but this woman was just so uncooperative. Granted, I was looking a bit scruffy these days... my hair was a shaggy shoulder length jungle cut without any styling or grooming products to control it. I had a cute stubble — or so I thought. And my limited wardrobe here at my parents' home didn't go beyond shorts and ganjis. But I had great legs — so why hide an asset? I had noticed her noticing them, when we met at the food truck that arrived at the gate every second day. I wanted to tell her the vendor did have far more interesting snacks than banana chips... but it was none of my business. Maybe her girls were addicted to banana chips. Weird!

Something was a little odd in that set up, but I couldn't put my finger on it. The husband was polite and 'normal'. She was definitely a little off. The girls were so spontaneous and sweet. While I sipped the beer I didn't really want, the girls asked whether they could come over and play with our cats later. We had three beautiful cats and the old folks loved to show them off. I looked around their home searching for clues... I was not getting something. What was that 'something'? I thought of my parent's home, and my own apartment — both places were neat and welcoming. This place was... I don't know how to put it... but it lacked something. Something major. And the husband's behaviour while being civil, was guarded and far from relaxed. Sterile and soulless — this house. Maybe their lives too. Except for the girls, who were natural and bouncy little things. Thank God my only child was a boy! What would I have done with a little girl? I'd seen the behaviour of these two over the past few weeks. Man... I would have messed up big time had I been stuck with a daughter!

When the girls came over to meet the cats, my mother was nervous. So was my father — even more nervous. The girls were wearing masks and gloves and their nanny, too was well-protected. They had followed the protocol, sanitized their hands and were making sure to stay six feet away from us. Despite these precautions, my mother called me to the other room, next to the living room, and whispered, 'These kids could be carriers... remember, we are very vulnerable, your father and I. Do you want us to get infected and die?'

I was a bit surprised to hear her speak like this. It was out of character. Besides, my baba was so thrilled to have company, and the nannies were busy having their own party in the kitchen. Seeing that the old folks were getting jittery, I told the children to play in the porch. Maybe that was a huge mistake — now when I look back at what happened next.

There we were, the bachchas and I, playing bat-ball in the narrow road, in front of the row of garages where our cars were generally parked. The security guards were relaxing on plastic chairs on either side, with checked handkerchiefs covering half their faces. All of a sudden, I spotted a biker turning in — one of the residents who had stepped out to get essentials. Nobody had noticed a small pool of oil on the rough ground, left by a car that had moved out of the garage for the first time in three months. Frankly, I am not at all sure — everything happened so swiftly. The biker slipped and swerved as his motorcycle skidded and came sliding to where I was playing with the three kids.

I reacted swiftly — thank God! And hurled myself in front of the machine that was inches away from the three bachchas. The rider was flung off and I saw his helmet flying as if in slo-mo. All I know is, the bike fell over my left leg while I shoved the kids away with my right arm, using as much force as my squash toned biceps could muster. I heard the three of them scream… as the nannies came running out of the kitchen, their mouths full of food and Mummyji shouted for help as loudly as she could, given her frail health and the state of her lungs. The old man also hobbled out of his arm chair, forgetting his arthritis momentarily and called the watchmen on duty, gesturing to get me out from under that still purring, burning hot Royal Enfield. The rider was limping up to see if we were okay. My sweet little baba was jumping up and down in excitement and clapping wildly, along with the girls.

Miss La Di Da rushed out at that precise moment, her abs

gleaming and on full display in a cute crop top after a hard yoga session. She had forgotten to wear her mask in her hurry. Her mouth was luscious. It was the first time I was seeing it. Even in that condition, when I didn't know whether or not my bones were broken, I wanted to tell her she looked hotter than Malaika. I think I gasped — not sure — but I definitely reacted like a moron. Miss La Di Da did not gasp. Nor did she smile. But her eyes softened momentarily. I noticed she did not rush to gather her girls and flounce off. She stayed. I grinned and said 'Hey!' She said 'Hey!' back. I knew home schooling was going to be fun from tomorrow.

A QUEST ENDS

I told my wife, 'It's okay... so what? I have you... you have me. I am happy in our small world. You also learn to be happy... we have everything! What's missing?' I should not have asked the last question at all! Because I already knew the answer. I could have bitten my tongue off, but the words were out! And Sushmita's eyes overflowed with tears. So did mine. When my wife cried, I also cried. It has always been this way. Since the day we met six and a half years ago, on 5th September. I remember everything! My memory is good. Hers is super good!

Both of us work in banking. I never use the phrase, 'We are bankers' because that is incorrect and misleading. We were at one of those typical networking dinners at Oberoi Hotel, where everybody knows everybody, which can get too boring. She was with a fancy foreign bank, and I had stayed with my original Indian bank from which my father had retired, even though many foreign banks had offered me a job. My friend Atul, who is quite the Romeo, introduced us to each other and

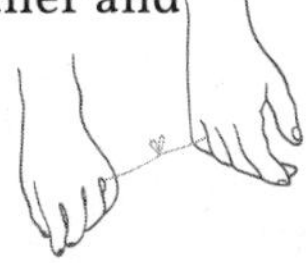

we clicked immediately. I thought Atul wanted to lagao a line himself. But maybe I was wrong.

I said to myself, 'Good, smart girl. Not that flirty type, who drops her saree pallu and keeps talking ankhon ankhon mein to seniors — meaning, influential men who can further her career. I noticed men also didn't take a 'chance' with her. She must have noticed some things about me, too, because she joined our small group at the dinner table and started chatting. She asked if I was going to attend next week's 'Banker of the Year' Awards function, adding excitedly, 'I hear the F.M. is coming to the event.'

Frankly, I had not been invited, but I said 'Definitely!' Through Atul, I managed an invite somehow. This is how we kept meeting and chatting. Soon our friends noticed our friendship and suggested we date. Why not? We went out a few times, here and there — coffee —shoffee, movies-popcorn, and then I proposed, after talking to my parents and disclosing all details — her salary, address, education, family background, community. My parents were satisfied. So were hers after meeting me at 'Sea Lounge', where we ate bhel and sandwiches. Our marriage was celebrated two months later, dhoom dhaam se, at Oberoi only — Regal Room. Lots of top bankers attended and gave good gifts. We had spared no expenses — achcha sa bar, multi-cuisine buffet, proper flower arrangements. And then — it was back to work! She in her bank, me in mine!

We both liked our jobs a lot. All our friends came from the same background, and we often travelled together — short trips, long trips. My wife and I enjoyed game parks and wildlife safaris. I had turned into a pretty good photographer, and had had a couple of exhibitions at good galleries. My website was popular with wildlife enthusiasts, and our next trip to South Africa had been booked well in advance — when, suddenly, the lockdown was declared.

I think Sushmita was rather relieved. She had not been keen on this trip from the beginning. She had told me, 'I feel we should be spending more time with each other than on taking pictures of lions and giraffes.' This was most unlike her! 'Should I cancel?' I asked, hoping she would say 'no'. But Sushmita had kept quiet and changed the subject. I knew what was troubling her — I didn't have to say it. Nor did I need to ask her. See, our main problem was we did not have a baby. That was the chief reason for the tears — hers and mine.

We had tried everything — from going to Godmen, fasting, following Chinese and Japanese techniques to conceive, and of course, visiting fertility clinics. All our tests were clear — totally fine! Still — no baby. Month after month after month, we had to go through the same tension. While all around us, our family and friends were having babies phataphat. First my younger sister had a boy, then Sushmita's older sister also had a boy (that too, after marrying later). Sushmita felt it more than I did.

Each time we met strangers who asked, 'How many children do you have?' she would turn to me and then say stiffly, 'We are consolidating our careers at this point... what's the hurry?'

This line worked for the first five years of our marriage. Till then even our parents and relatives were understanding. They would nod their heads and say, 'Young people today live in a different world. Their lives are so busy — work, work, work! Where is the time for children? But there will be good news very soon...' This was far from the truth. Sushmita and I had wanted a baby in the second year itself. Yes, during the first year, we wanted to enjoy our life together, continue the honeymoon (Oh and what a honeymoon! We went to Ranthambore. Expensive, it was. But such a treat. And how lucky we were to see tigers on all four days!). Our lives were set, we'd attend parties, socialise, travel... these were the 'luxuries' our parents never enjoyed. But with our combined salaries, we had enough to spend on all the things we wanted — without getting stressed over big bills.

Sushmita and I have always been in perfect sync. She is careful with money and so am I. But of the two, I think I am the one who is over emotional, over sentimental. 'Softy', she calls me. In fact, that's the nickname she gave me on our wedding night itself when I cried more than her during the bidhai ceremony. I call her 'Sushi' — we both enjoy eating sushi since our favourite cuisine is Japanese!

We are now in the sixth year of our marriage, and following the international WFH protocol. It is not too tough, since we are both disciplined and work systematically. But because we spend so much time together, doing everything saath-saath — washing clothes, ironing, cooking, cleaning and swabbing, there are times when we miss that 'other thing', our own baby.

Though we never talk about it. Sushi says there is no point. We have tried our best — here and abroad. Sent all our test results to the top fertility experts, changed our diet to a more alkaline one, followed the fertility cycle closely each month — what more? I have even left my bank abruptly half-way through a meeting to rush home, because Sushi called to say the best time to attempt a baby was between 2.30 pm and 3 pm. Imagine my tension! We were frank with each other, like that. How was it possible to perform mechanically, when I could only see balance sheets in front of my eyes?

Sushi was understanding — and after all, this was a joint venture. We would watch porn... and wait for something to happen. Sometimes I got an erection, sometimes, I didn't. Sushi never blamed me, but I could see the disappointment in her eyes. Those eyes used to cloud over and remain sad for days. We would eat our meals in silence and I knew she could think of nothing else... but our baby.

Frankly, I didn't mind the WFH routine at all. Sushi and I had established a comfortable pattern and there were no complaints from anybody. She had her workspace and I had mine. She preferred the living room, and I liked our balcony with a fantastic view of the Race Course. We relaxed in the evenings — something we never found the time to do before the lockdown. We lounged in bed, watching our favourite shows like 'The Crown' or reruns of 'Downton Abbey' sometimes, we watched old Bengali films or Hindi films. We both admired Bimal Roy, so that was great. As it is, we hardly fought — our views were same-to-same on most topics.

Except on our Prime Minister. Of course, I was upset by his demonetization policy, but not half as much as Sushi. We had decided not to argue — why fight over Narendra Modi, when there were better subjects to discuss?

We valued our precious time together these days. We realised it was a time that may never come back again. We listened to interesting, motivational talks and took online classes to learn new skills — how to play the flute, how to roll the perfect sushi, how to exercise in the correct manner without a personal trainer, how to appreciate fine wine... we even joined online ballroom dancing groups to learn how to foxtrot! Fortunately, our families were keeping well, no Covid scares, and our building society was extra cautious. We were not anxious about the future ourselves — we had enough for our needs. This flat was ours. The cars were fully paid up. And... we didn't have a baby to plan a future for.

I would often joke with Sushi, 'Why take tension for nothing? Look at our friends — so much tension! And now their children are at home the whole day creating a toofan and not obeying them. Thank God we don't have all that.' Sushi would change the subject immediately and pick up a book I knew she was not going to read.

After a lot of thinking, I plucked up enough courage one afternoon, and asked Sushi an important question. She was serving me a cold soup called Gazpacho she had watched being made on her favourite 'easy-to-make-recipes' site. She had told me it was a Spanish soup that Spanish people enjoyed in summer. I took my time before uttering these words, 'What about... I'm just saying... I was thinking... what about adopting a little one? I have been doing some solid research... solid! You don't have to answer just now... but...'

I was afraid to look into her eyes. I knew if she cried, I would also cry. There was silence. I was staring into my soup bowl. I had never tasted cold soup before. I always thought soup was served hot. Anyway, I didn't want to hurt Sushi's feelings — what if I didn't like it? She had taken a lot of trouble to make it in advance and chill it in the fridge. By God! I was so nervous, so nervous! The question was out. I could not take my words back. I waited. I think I had stopped breathing.

I was still staring into the soup bowl when I felt Sushi's hand on my shoulder. She had come around the table, and was behind me, I was sure she was crying. And didn't want me to cry as well. I turned around to comfort her... stammering, 'I'm so sorry... it was just a suggestion. Please don't be angry...'

And then... before I could utter another word, I heard Sushi say clearly, in a strong voice, 'I have a name for our daughter — we will call her "Anwesha" — it means "quest". With her in our life, our quest will finally be over.' After that, we both cried. Nicely. And thoroughly enjoyed Sushi's cold soup.

OPEN LETTER TO A MICROBE

Dear Corona Uncle,

I am a 10 year old girl, and I just want to tell you to go away forever. You have been very, very evil, and it is about time you left our beautiful world. We have all suffered and suffered for so many months. I watch the news on television and see innocent people dying every day. I also see my mummy-papa struggling like anything. I see all the people around me also suffering so much because of you. First, we thought you were not real. We believed everyone when they said you may not come to India at all!

I asked my papa, 'Is that possible, that Corona uncle will fly over our heads and land far away?' My papa didn't reply immediately, but he was definitely looking worried and talking in a serious way to my mama, and later to grandma and grandpa. I asked him to show me a picture of corona — I wanted to see the monster, you, for myself. He showed me something on his phone which looked like a party decoration.

I said to my papa, 'coronavirus looks like a fluffy little ball... so sweet!' And he explained you were not sweet at all, and that you were here, there, everywhere getting inside our bodies, deep into our lungs, and killing us. corona Uncle — you are a murderer. I hate you! The whole world hates you! You had better leave before Diwali and Christmas, when we all like to have fun, exchange gifts, light patakas, eat yummy food and decorate a tree with fairy lights and streamers. As it is, we kids have not been to any birthday party for over three months — just imagine what we are feeling! Even my own birthday party was celebrated sitting in the house, without friends! Papa had baked a cake and tried to make my room look happy and nice with left over streamers from my school project. I know everybody had tried their best to make me happy, but I had cried and cried! No new dress on my birthday! No treats and no friends there as I cut my cake. No friends were there to sing 'Happy Birthday' loudly. When I saw that one, small little candle on the cake, I felt really bad... there should have been ten lovely candles and lots of fun with friends — not this sort of party with just the three of us posing for selfies. Even the Zoom call with my school friends was a flop and made me cry even more! I am an only child, so that is another thing — I feel very lonely. Mummy-Papa work nonstop, and are on their computers , talking and talking and talking to office people, till late at night. What am I supposed to do while they work?

Thank God, these last few days, their mood has been better. Mummy says her business is picking up slowly. Papa also smiles more and drinks less coffee than before. They sit and talk nicely at the dining table, which makes me feel so happy!

They include me in their conversation, which they never used to do earlier. I have started watering our plants, and told Mummy it is my duty from now on. I also set the table and try and keep my toys and books away without bothering my parents. Of course, I hate home schooling, and I know they also hate it, but there is no other choice. I feel bad for my teachers who work very hard to make all of us listen to them and do our work on time. I am dying to go back to my school and play with my friends again. I don't mind studying really hard, if I have friends to study with. I don't even mind getting punished for not doing my school work properly, if I am with everybody else, laughing and running here and there. Corona Uncle... when will our schools open?

Once you leave our world, we will look after it properly and not be careless. You have taught us a lesson, Corona Uncle. When I water the plants in our small terrace garden these days, I feel so nice, because I see how little green shoots have started to come out of the moist soil. One little hibiscus bloomed for the first time, and I gave it to Ganeshji and told him to look after all of us. The sky from the window looks so pretty and blue, like in our holiday pictures from hill stations. Mummy is breathing better, so is grandma, because they don't need to use the asthma pump. Things are improving slowly, even I am changing... but I need a little time! I have promised Mummy-Papa I won't keep pestering them to order pizzas and burgers, pizzas and burgers. Both of them have taken so much trouble to make food for all of us — I have started liking ghar ka khana for the first time ever! Anyway... it is time to say 'Goodbye' to you. Go awayyyyyyyyy! And never come back!!

I am wishing everyone in advance, because I am sure this year we will burn the wicked Corona Uncle, not just Ravan, on the last day of Dussehra. Once we destroy both, there will be diyas and diyas and diyas everywhere... I am looking forward to new clothes... new everything! Happy Diwali, world.

Yours Sincerely,
Shanti

Acknowledgements

Two days before one of India's greatest painters, M.F. Husain, died at the Royal Brompton Hospital in London on 9th June 2011, I was at his bedside, listening to him attentively as he spoke at length in his characteristic soft voice, his expressive, restless hands gesturing to make a point. He was 95 years old, and may have known he didn't have long to live. But you'd never have guessed it, going by the conversation that late evening. He was busy making plans for his next exhibition... and the next. Plans that covered ten years. There was zero self-doubt and not a trace of regret. Husain Saab had no time for the past — his vast creative energy was reserved for the future.

It was our last meeting. I saw him next at the funeral.

That's life.

Why am I referring to him today as I write? Because I want to acknowledge the profound impact he had on my life. And the inspiration that the last conversation — those last few words — provided. When the punishing lockdown was announced,

I asked myself what would Husain Saab have done during the pandemic? The answer was obvious — he would have picked up his paintbrush and gone to work.

With that image in mind to guide me, I picked up my pen and started writing. It is this book that emerged.

And then came the best news of all — I sent the first few stories to Himanjali Sankar at Simon & Schuster India, for a quick dekho. It was more a hesitant 'What do you think?' gesture. Himanjali thought. I guess, she liked. And — *Lockdown Liaisons* — took flight. It was an exciting new platform for me, and we were keen to explore its potential. My agent, Kanishka Gupta jumped in enthusiastically... and so began the adventure! The format fell into place and my writing was forced to keep pace — ha! What an exciting race! That was the fun part.

A big shout out to the design and digital team at Simon & Schuster India... Mridu, Abhay. And to the international artist, Viveek Sharma, for his evocative cover image.

To my family. I could not have survived the lockdown without all of you — Dilip Dé, Anandita and Gong Li who suffered 'house arrest' along with me. Aditya, Avantikka and Arundhati, who offered virtual encouragement from their homes. So near... and yet so far. Everything. Everyone.

And most of all, the biggest hug to my dining table — my steady and sturdy companion throughout the pandemic. Thank you, for providing solid support!